The Ordinary Princess

The Ordinary Princess

Written and Illustrated by

M. M. KAYE

VIKING

VIKING

Published by the Penguin Group

Penguin Putnam Books for Young Readers,

345 Hudson Street, New York, New York 10014, U.S.A.

Penguin Books Ltd, 80 Strand, London WC2R 0RL, England

Penguin Books Australia Ltd, Ringwood, Victoria, Australia

Penguin Books Canada Ltd, 10 Alcorn Avenue, Toronto, Ontario, Canada M4V 3B2

Penguin Books (N.Z.) Ltd, 182-190 Wairau Road, Auckland 10, New Zealand

Penguin Books Ltd, Registered Offices: Harmondsworth, Middlesex, England

First published in Great Britain in 1980 by Kestrel

First published in the United States in 1980 by Doubleday & Company, Inc.

This edition published in 2002 by Viking, a division of Penguin Putnam Books for Young Readers.

3 5 7 9 10 8 6 4 2

LIBRARY OF CONGRESS CATALOGING-IN-PUBLICATION DATA

Kaye, M.M. (Mary Margaret), 1911–

The ordinary princess / written and illustrated by M.M. Kaye

p. cm.

Summary: At her christening, a princess is given the gift of "ordinariness" by a fairy,

and the consequences of that eventually take her to a nearby palace where, as the

fourteenth assistant kitchen maid, she meets the prince for her.

ISBN 0-670-03544-0

[1. Princesses—Fiction. 2. Fairy tales.] I. Title.

PZ8. K28 Or 2002

Fic—dc21   2001026545

Printed in U.S.A.

For
my granddaughter
Mollie Miranda Kaye

Contents

The Ordinary Princess

Foreword by the Author

This story was written many moons ago under an apple tree in an orchard in Kent, which is one of England's prettiest counties.

It was springtime and I was staying with a school friend whose parents owned an old manor house that was full of pictures and books: books for grown-ups and books for children. Among the latter I was delighted to discover some that I knew well; for I had once had a whole set of these myself, only to lose them when a London warehouse, in which most of our family belongings had been stored after my father died, caught fire and burned to the ground.

They were the Andrew Lang fairy books, which Lang had compiled from stories that he had collected from all over the world. From China and India, Persia and Arabia, France, Britain and Spain, Germany, Russia and the Netherlands, and, in fact, from anywhere where generations of people have told their children fairy tales at bedtime—which means practically everywhere!

Nowadays *The Blue Fairy Book*, *The Green Fairy Book*, *The Lilac Fairy Book*, and so on, right through the list of colors, are collector's items that fetch high prices at book auctions. Their charming illustrations were mostly the work of an artist called H. J. Ford, and I had admired them so much, particularly the colored ones, that I had made up my mind at a very early age that I too would be an illustrator of children's books when I grew up.

During the next few days I reread most of them, and it was only after I had read at least twenty of the stories that I noticed something that had never struck me before—I suppose because I had always taken it for granted. All the princesses, apart from such rare exceptions as Snow White, were blond, blue-eyed, and beautiful, with lovely figures and complexions and extravagantly long hair. This struck me as most unfair, and suddenly I began to wonder just how many handsome young princes would have asked a king for the hand of his daughter if that daughter had happened to be gawky, snub-nosed, and freckled, with shortish mouse-colored hair? None, I suspected. They would all have been off chasing after some lissome Royal Highness with large blue eyes and yards of golden hair and probably nothing whatever between her ears!

It was in that moment that a story about a princess who turned out to be ordinary jumped into my mind, and the very next morning I took my pencil box and a large rough-notebook down to the orchard and, having settled myself under an apple tree in full bloom, began to write it. England was having a marvelous spring that year, and the day was warm and windless and without a cloud in the sky. A perfect day and a perfect place to write a fairy story. For what could be a better spot for a princess—even an ordinary one—to be born in than an apple orchard in spring?

Apart from the fact that it was my hand that scribbled it all down, I cannot honestly claim to have written her story, for in fact it wrote itself. And at such breakneck speed that it was all I could do to make my pencil keep up with the tale that my head was telling me. It was an experience that has only happened to me on one other occasion, and I only wish it would happen more often, since except for those two occasions I am an extremely slow writer. Snails are not in the same league with me, and I always write in pencil so that I can rub out my mistakes. Yet I cannot remember using my eraser even once when I was writing *The Ordinary Princess*, and I sometimes think that Amy herself must have been doing the dictating. If so, she couldn't spell any better than I can. I never could spell. And still can't, worse luck!

When the story stopped of its own accord, I copied it out tidily from my rough-notebook onto lined paper, and once I was back again at work in London, a friend typed it out for me. After that, whenever I had any spare time, I would do one of the illustrations for it. The trouble was that I never had much spare time in those days, and that is why the manuscript, and as many of the illustrations as I had managed to do, eventually got put away in a portfolio and forgotten.

It is nice to know that at long last it is seeing the light of day, and I hope very much that readers will enjoy it. For if a time ever comes when children turn up their noses at such things as fairy tales and Father Christmas and Halloween, the world will be a lot duller—and not nearly such a nice place to live in!

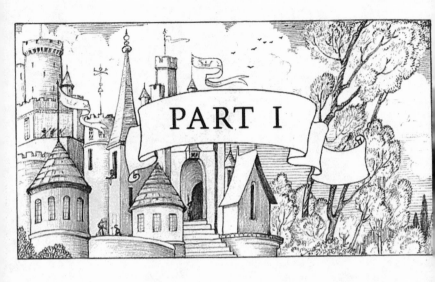

PART I

Lavender's Blue

How It Began

Long and long ago, when Oberon was king of the fairies, there reigned over the fair country of Phantasmorania a monarch who had six beautiful daughters.

They were in every way all that real princesses should be, for their hair was as yellow as the gold that is mined by the little gnomes in the mountains of the north, their eyes were as blue as the larkspurs in the palace gardens, and they had complexions like wild rose petals and cream.

Their royal Mama the Queen was very proud of them, and they had all had extremely grand christenings when they were babies. She had called them all after precious stones and was often heard to refer to them playfully as "my jewels." Their names were Diamond, Opal, Emerald, Sapphire, Crystal and Pearl.

Every princess wore a golden crown set with the jewels of her first name, so you can imagine the excitement in the city of Phanff (which is the capital of Phantasmorania) when the news leaked out that Messrs. Heibendiks & Piphorn, Goldsmiths and Silversmiths, By Appointment to His Majesty King Hulderbrand, had been commissioned to make another crown and this time to set it with amethysts.

"So there is going to be a seventh princess at the palace," exclaimed the housewives of Phanff.

"That is as it should be; a seventh daughter is always lucky," cackled the oldest inhabitant.

"A seventh princess!" sighed the romantic maidens. "And of course she will be the most beautiful of all. Youngest princesses always are."

"How lucky she will be!" And "Oh, how lovely to be a princess," thought the schoolchildren, looking enviously across the roofs of the town to where the tall towers and pointed turrets of the Royal Palace of Phanff rose high above the treetops.

"How do you know that it won't be a prince this time?" asked the travelers stopping at the inns and taverns of the city. But the townspeople and the innkeepers and the hosts of the taverns only laughed and said, "It is plain that you are strangers to the country. Our royal family always has princesses."

"But you have a king," objected the travelers.

"Ah yes; but by tradition the heir to the throne is always the youngest son of the eldest princess. It's very simple."

And so, upon a lovely spring morning, when the primroses were gold in the Forest of Faraway and the woods were white with wild cherry blossom, the great bronze cannon on the palace walls, which is only fired at the birth of a royal baby, boomed out on the still air. And as the first puff of smoke broke from the walls and the first *"Boom!"* rang out over the city, the townspeople stopped their work and housewives, shopkeepers and schoolchildren all ran out together into the streets.

Every eye was turned to the palace. *"Boom!"* rang out the cannon. *"Boom!"* *"Boom!"* "Fifteen — sixteen — seventeen — eighteen — nineteen," counted the townsfolk. "Twenty! A princess!" they cried. And they threw their hats in the air and cheered while the bells of all the churches in the city rang a merry peal and a general holiday was declared in honor of the occasion.

In a rich and splendid room, high up in a turret of the palace, the cause of all the excitement and rejoicing lay in a golden cradle and blinked at the carved ceiling.

The seventh princess really was the loveliest baby imaginable. She was no bigger than one of her sisters' dolls, but she was as pink and white and gold as the apple blossoms and the spring sunshine, and her eyes were as blue as the sky above the Forest of Faraway. Her nurses and ladies-in-waiting never tired of admiring and exclaiming over her many perfections, and from the first she was a very good-tempered baby. She never cried or screamed but would lie on her back and smile at the sunbeams dancing on the ceiling, or sleep for hours on end.

She had a very grand nursery for such a very small person, for the ceiling was all carved and painted with legends of the Forest of Faraway, and the walls were hung with amethyst-colored tapestry. The floor was spread with silken carpets, and the seventh princess had no less than twelve attendants all her own. First there was her nurse, Marta, then three under-nurses, two ladies-in-waiting, four nurserymaids, and two pages. Sometimes the pages would play on flutes and viols while the ladies-in-waiting sang lullabies to hush the seventh princess to sleep.

When she was six weeks old, preparations were begun for an especially grand and splendid christening. Hundreds of clerks sat at ivory desks all day, writing out invitations with gold ink on parchment. Hundreds of pages heated gold sealing wax to seal the envelopes, and hundreds of the King's messengers put spurs to their horses and rode away east and

west and north and south to deliver them to the invited guests.

The list of invitations was so long that it took the Lord High Chamberlain from before breakfast until after suppertime to read it, while the roll it made was so large that it took six men-at-arms to carry it. There had been a long debate in Council on "The Advisability of Inviting Fairies to the Christening." The King had been against it from the first, but he had ended by being overruled by the Queen, who had been backed up by the Prime Minister and the Lord High Chamberlain and a large majority of the councillors.

"Oh, all right—have it your own way," said the King at last. "But mind you, I think it's *rash*. And I shall go on saying that it's rash. We didn't have any of these fairy nuisances at the christenings of my other daughters, and what happened?"

"Nothing," said the Queen.

"Precisely," said the King. "Perfect peace and quiet. Everything went off beautifully; no fuss or bother and everyone had an extremely good time."

"But Your Majesty—" began the Prime Minister.

"I know, I know. Don't interrupt me," said the King testily. "You are going to tell me that it is the custom of our kingdom to invite all fairies to the christening of a seventh daughter. You have already said it at least seven times, and I still say that it's rash!"

"There is no need to get heated about it, dear," said the Queen. "You know perfectly well that it has always been done before and that it would look very odd if it were not done now."

"I'm not getting heated," said the King. "I only said that it was rash."

H·M QUEEN RODEHESIA

"For goodness' sake, Hulderbrand," snapped the Queen, almost losing her royal temper, "do stop using that annoying word." She took a deep breath and recovered her queenly calm: "Besides, dear, think how useful it will be. Fairies always give such delightful presents. Like Good Temper and—and Unfailing Charm and Unfading Beauty. You wouldn't want to deprive your daughter of such a chance?"

"I can only repeat," said the King stubbornly, "that to invite fairies to a christening is asking for trouble. And getting it," he added gloomily. "Speaking for myself," said the King, "I'd far rather ask several man-eating tigers. *You* may have forgotten what happened to my great-great-great-grandmother, but I have not. Had to sleep for a hundred years, poor girl, and the entire court with her, and all because of some silly fairy-business at the christening."

"But Your Majesty forgets," put in the Prime Minister, "that the unfortunate episode you refer to was due to gross neglect and carelessness. History tells us that an influential fairy was not invited. But on this occasion I, personally, will take the greatest possible care that no such calamity occurs again." And the Prime Minister tried to look very uncareless indeed.

The Lord High Chamberlain hastened to add that no single member of King Oberon's court would be omitted from the list of guests: "And we must not forget," he pointed out, "that as Her Majesty has said, these—er—persons have it in their power to bestow the most valuable of gifts. For your daughter's sake—" urged the Lord High Chamberlain.

"Oh, all right, all right," said the King peevishly. "Don't let's go over all that again. But you mark my words," he said, "I'd much rather have a nice silver-plated christening mug from a nice solid baron than some chancy thing like Unfading Beauty from a tricky creature with wings and a wand! Besides," said the King, "who's to tell that some tiresome fairy won't get out on the wrong side of her bed that day and give my daughter Perpetual Bad Temper instead? Answer me that!"

"*Really,* Hulderbrand," sighed the Queen in an exasperated sort of voice, "I find you quite impos-

sible at times. It seems to me that you are determined to be unreasonable about the whole affair."

"But Your Majesty—" began the Prime Minister.

"But Your Majesty—" began the Lord High Chamberlain.

"But Your Majesty—" chorused the councillors.

"Oh, all right," said the King. "Have it your own
way. Ask the lot. Don't mind me!" He gathered up
his train and glared at his councillors, the Prime
Minister, the Lord High Chamberlain, and the
Queen. "But don't say I didn't warn you," he said.
"No fairies have ever attended a christening without
some funny business happening somewhere. You
just mark my words," said the King. "It's rash."

And with that he bounced out of the Council
chamber and slammed the door behind him.

So the fairies were invited after all, and the most
tremendous care was taken that no fairy should be
overlooked: in fact a special committee was ap-
pointed to see to it that no one was forgotten. As the
day of the christening approached, the whole palace
buzzed with bustle and excitement like a hive of
bees.

In the royal kitchens two hundred and twenty
cooks, four hundred scullions, as many servingmen,
and five hundred kitchen maids worked like mad,
baking cakes and pies and pastries. They stuffed
swans and peacocks and boars' heads and made wonderful sweets—marzipan trees hung with crystalized
cherries, and castles and dragons and great ships of
sugar candy. Five cooks from Italy worked on the
christening cake, which was decorated with

hundreds of sugar bells and crystalized roses, and was so tall that they had to stand on silver stepladders to ice it.

Ladies-in-waiting filled golden flower vases and crystal bowls with hundreds of blooms, so that the whole palace looked like a flower garden and smelled most deliciously of roses and lilies and lilac. Housemaids polished the chandeliers, and footmen and pages ran to and fro with trays full of china and glass. In the city the rich merchants and important citizens who had been invited to the ceremony were having new suits and dresses made for the occasion, and the townsfolk were preparing bonfires and decorating their streets and houses with banners and wreaths.

The day of the christening dawned bright and sunny, with not a single cloud in the blue sky. Guns boomed and church bells rang in every steeple as the townsfolk crowded round the palace to cheer the arrival of the guests. But the seventh princess was quite unbothered by all this noise and fuss. She lay in her magnificent cradle in the great throne room and stared at the dangling fringe of little golden bells on the canopy above her head and paid no attention to the guests at all.

She had seven godfathers and seventeen godmothers, and when the christening ceremony was over, heralds in scarlet and gold blew a fanfare on silver trumpets and announced her seven names to the populace:

"Her Serene and Royal Highness the Princess

Amethyst Alexandra Augusta Araminta Adelaide Aurelia Anne!" cried the heralds.

Then all the people cheered and flung their hats into the air, and a thousand white doves were released from the windows of the palace. The doves flew out into the sunshine and circled and cooed above the tall turrets and battlements before winging their way into the Forest of Faraway. While inside the throne room the guests passed in procession by the cradle, each in turn presenting a christening gift to the seventh princess.

The presents mounted up in a huge pile until they almost reached the ceiling, but the gifts that the fairies gave took up no room at all, for the sort of presents *they* give do not need to be packed in boxes.

They gave the seventh princess Charm and Wit and Grace and Courage, and a great many other things like that, and the Queen could not help looking extremely pleased with herself and saying in a rather loud whisper to the King, "You see it has all turned out a great success in spite of all your fussing. I told you so."

But the King only sniffed. "I wouldn't speak too soon," he said pessimistically. "There's still a lot of time for something nasty to happen."

And just then, something did.

The last and most important of the fairy godmothers had arrived late because of a traffic jam on the road to the palace. Her name was Crustacea, and she was the fairy-in-charge-of-water, which means that she was the head fairy of all the seas, pools, ponds, lakes and rivers.

She was very old and rather deaf, and her temper was always inclined to be a little uncertain when she was on dry land. But for all that, she was a very powerful and important lady, and all the guests made way for her as she hobbled up to the cradle.

The Queen bowed most graciously to her, and the King muttered something about being pleased to see her, while the old fairy peered at them over the top of her horn-rimmed spectacles.

"I wish," said the old fairy crossly, "that people who give large parties would take the trouble to see that the traffic is properly controlled. Your police appear to be quite useless. Would you believe it, I was held up in a crush of carriages for over half an hour? *Me!* At *my* age!! I cannot endure dust and I am almost as dry as a bone!"

And indeed her long seaweedy robe was hardly damp, instead of nice and seawatery as she liked it.

The Queen was full of apologies and sent out at once for a bowl of salt water from the royal fish ponds.

Old Crustacea poured some of it over herself and drank the rest and said she felt better. The water trickled down her seaweedy robe and made messy pools on the polished floor, but nobody liked to mention it.

"And now," said old Crustacea, "let's have a look at this brat of yours."

She hobbled up to the cradle and peered down at the seventh princess.

The seventh princess had been snoozing, but now she opened one blue eye, and then the other, and she smiled at the old fairy.

Old Crustacea put out a long bony finger and touched the seventh princess's pink cheek. Then she looked at the King and Queen and the resplendent guests and the six little sister princesses, each more beautiful than the last, and finally she looked at the huge pile of glittering presents and the list that the Lord High Chamberlain had made of the gifts bestowed by the other fairies.

"Hmm!" said the Fairy Crustacea. "Wit, Charm, Courage, Health, Wisdom, Grace . . . Good gracious,

poor child! Well, thank goodness my magic is stronger than anyone else's."

She raised her twisty coral stick and waved it three times over the cradle of the seventh princess. "My child," said the Fairy Crustacea, "I am going to give you something that will probably bring you more happiness than all these fal-lals and fripperies put together. You shall be Ordinary!"

And nodding her head briskly the Fairy Crustacea turned away and hobbled rapidly out of the throne room, leaning on her twisty coral stick and leaving a faint smell of seaweed and a damp track on the polished floor behind her.

For quite a minute after she had gone there was a stunned silence in the red and gold throne room of the palace. It was broken by the King.

"I told you so!" said the King triumphantly. "Rash," said the King. "I *knew* it was rash. Didn't I say that something like this was bound to happen?"

Words cannot describe the scene that followed. The Queen wept, and the King went on saying, "Rash," and "I told you so," until the Prime Minister felt like resigning on the spot. Everybody talked at once, words like "Impossible!" "Horrors!" and "Disgraceful!" flew in all directions, and the noise became so great that you could hardly have heard yourself think.

It was then that the seventh princess proceeded to show how quickly the Fairy Crustacea's gift had worked.

She screwed up her apple-blossom face into something that resembled a small squashed tomato, and, opening her mouth as wide as possible, she screamed

and screamed—as any ordinary baby would have
done after a tiring day and with all that noise going
on.

Everybody stopped talking at once and rushed forward to the cradle. But the seventh princess just kept
right on screaming. She didn't like all these
strangers, she was tired and bored and hungry, and
she didn't care who knew it.

"Yaaaaaaa! Oooooooo! Gwwowow!" screamed
the seventh princess, doubling up her small pink
fists and turning quite purple in the face.

The Queen fainted away and had to be revived
with smelling salts. The King said, "I told you it was
rash," for the seventeenth time, and the Prime Minister resigned on the spot, while the Lord High
Chamberlain sent half a dozen gentlemen-in-waiting
hurrying after the Fairy Crustacea to beg her please
to come back and change her mind.

But alas! By the time the panting messengers
reached the gates, the Fairy Crustacea had gone.

So that was that.

The christening party broke up in confusion and
the guests said good-bye, and how sorry they were,
but perhaps it wouldn't turn out to be so bad after
all, one must look on the bright side, mustn't one,
and all the other gifts were very beautiful and—er—
gratifying, so perhaps . . .

The last coach of the last guest rumbled out of the
palace yard, and the footmen and pages and servingmen began to clear away the remnants of the feast.
They took the leftover cakes and pastries and the
broken bits of marzipan trees, sugar-candy castles,
and ships and dragons home to their friends and re-

lations, while the Queen took to her bed in a state of nervous prostration and the Prime Minister took to his with a headache.

But as for Her Serene and Royal Highness the Princess Amethyst Alexandra Augusta Araminta Adelaide Aurelia Anne of Phantasmorania, she was taken back to her royal nursery still screaming as determinedly as ever.

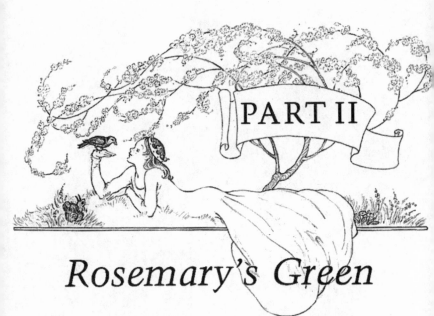

PART II

Rosemary's Green

Amy

Long sunny years drifted by in the kingdom of Phantasmorania. And with every passing year the old Fairy Crustacea's gift became more and more noticeable, as the seventh princess became more and more ordinary.

No one ever called her by her grand name now. From the townsfolk in the city down to the smallest page at the palace, she was always known simply as "the Ordinary Princess," while even her own family never called her Amethyst. They called her Amy. And what could be more ordinary than that?

After the day of her christening, she had begun to change from a beautiful baby princess into just an ordinary baby. Her soft golden curls stopped curling and became darker, and her blue eyes turned a grayish-brown neither-here-nor-there color. And as she

grew older, her little nose turned up and her hair hung down straighter and straighter, and not all the curlpapers in the world could make it look as a proper princess's should.

Her six lovely sisters, with their rose-petal complexions, their straight, white little noses, rippling golden hair and perfect deportment, were a delight to see. But Amy—! Oh dear, how ordinary she was!

Her Mama the Queen who was a very determined woman, would not give up hope that something could be done to correct the distressing ordinariness of her youngest daughter. She hired dancing masters from Spain to teach her elegance and deportment and hairdressers and beauty experts from France to improve her hair and complexion. But all to no avail.

Even the court magician was no use. His card, which he always carried with him, had printed in one corner, ALL KINDS OF CHARMS ON APPLICATION. VANISHING DONE. But none of his charms made any difference to the ordinariness of the Ordinary Princess, and in spite of his best efforts, not one single freckle ever vanished off the Princess Amy's little snub nose.

She grew up as gawky as possible, with a distressing habit of standing with her feet apart and her hands behind her back, and hair of a color that not even a court poet could describe as anything but just plain mouse. But though she proved every day how strong the old Fairy Crustacea's magic had been, her other christening gifts were not entirely wasted.

True, the splendid jewels and brocades of the kings and princes and barons were quite out of place on her homely little person, but the fairy gifts had been very useful, for though she was ordinary, she possessed health, wit, courage, charm, and cheerfulness. But because she was not beautiful, no one ever seemed to notice these other qualities, which is so often the way of the world. Not that it ever worried the Ordinary Princess.

She was sometimes sorry that she was such a disappointment to her royal Mama the Queen. "But after all," said the Ordinary Princess, "Mama has six perfectly scrumptious daughters, so I don't think that *one* not-so-goodish one ought to matter very much."

There were also times when (being a very ordinary sort of person) she felt a little envious of her sisters' beauty. "But oh! what a lot of fun they miss by not being me," said the Princess Amy as she leaned her elbows on the windowsill of her room and looked out over the forest. "They have to keep their complexions white and play the harp and embroider tapestry, and the only game they ever play is throwing each other a golden ball. But I do such exciting things!" said the Ordinary Princess. And she smiled a little secret smile to herself as she leaned far out of the window to sniff the breeze from the forest.

Her room was in one of the turrets on the palace wall, a big round room with tall pointed windows on three sides of it, so that from one window she could see the sunrise and from another the sunset. It was the same room in which she had lain as a baby in her golden cradle and blinked at the painted ceiling. Amethyst-colored tapestry still covered the walls, and outside the window grew a great wisteria hung with pale purple blossoms. The wisteria had

a strong twisty gray stem that climbed and clung to the old weather-beaten stones of the turret, and the Ordinary Princess smiled again as she leaned out and touched that rough knobbly stem with her little brown hand.

She shared a particular secret with the old wisteria

that nobody in the palace ever suspected—not even Nurse Marta.

Since the time when she was three years old she had always longed to escape from the palace gardens and play in the forest—the great, beautiful, mysterious Forest of Faraway that swept right up to the very walls of the palace. From her window she could watch the rabbits frolicking among the ferns and moss, and the shy deer picking their way through the leafy aisles between the tree trunks.

Then one summer evening, when she had been put to bed while it was still light outside, she had a great idea—a wonderful idea. It was so wonderful that she could not wait to carry it out, and the very next minute she was climbing out of her turret window and down the twisty curves of the old wisteria and had run off into the forest to play.

Since that first time, when she was little more than six years old, she had done it many, many times. The old wisteria became a ladder into her secret world, and almost every day, rain·or shine, she would scramble down the turret wall and be off into the forest, leaving her crown behind and tucking up her trailing dresses, and making believe that she was a peasant girl or a woodcutter's daughter, living alone in the greenwood.

The Forest of Faraway is surely the most beautiful place in the world. Between the great tree trunks the ground is carpeted with deep emerald moss, all starry with flowers. Countless wild birds build their nests there, and on moonlit nights in spring it is full of the song of many nightingales. No fierce animals ever roam there but only the dappled deer, the frolicsome rabbits, and little gentle woodland creatures. And sometimes in the spring you would think that the sky must have fallen into the forest, for thousands upon thousands of bluebells spread their sapphire carpets through the glades.

When March winds blow coldly over the city, inside the forest it is warm and still; and on hot summer days the forest glades are cool and green. Even on wintry or wet days it seemed beautiful to the Ordinary Princess, so while her six beautiful sisters played with their golden ball in the palace gardens, she played with the rabbits and the deer in the forest.

The six proper princesses never went out of doors without pages to carry silken canopies over their heads, for fear the sunshine might spoil their complexions. But the Ordinary Princess pushed her crown under the royal nightdress case and never wore a hat, and her nose got frecklier and frecklier in spite of all the Queen's lily lotions and lemon juice.

The six lovely princesses had ladies-in-waiting and pages standing around when they played ball, to pick it up when they dropped it. But the Ordinary Princess learned to climb trees like a squirrel and to swim like an otter in the deep forest pools. She had a lovely time!

Nobody could ever understand why she grew so brown or why her brocaded gowns were always getting torn and her embroidered shoes so stained and scratched. But then no one ever worried much about her anyway, and whenever anyone remembered to ask where she was, the answer was nearly always "Somewhere about." For to tell the truth, they were really all quite glad that she should keep out of the way, as such a very ordinary child was a disgrace to any royal family.

So it is not surprising that the courtiers sometimes forgot that there was a seventh princess at all.

One by one the six beautiful sisters grew up and married handsome and gallant princes. And six years running the Ordinary Princess followed one of her sisters down the long, dim aisle of the great cathedral of Phanff and helped to carry the bride's train and threw rice and rose petals after the glass coach as the bride and her groom drove away from the palace.

The sixth year she had to carry the train all by herself, for all the other sisters were married, so there was only herself to follow the Princess Pearl up the aisle when Pearl married the Crown Prince of Crystalvia.

The bride's train was of silver tissue embroidered with pearls, and as it was ten yards long, the Ordinary Princess found it exceedingly heavy and very difficult to manage.

It was a hot day and the cathedral was rather stuffy—what with the huge crowd of wedding guests, the clouds of incense from the swinging silver censers, the thousands of lighted candles and the heavy scent of lilies and white roses. The Princess Pearl looked lovelier than ever, and the Crown Prince of Crystalvia very handsome and gallant; though privately the Ordinary Princess thought him rather stiff. "He may be very good looking," she thought, "but I'm quite sure that he has never giggled one good giggle in his life!"

Her own bridesmaid's dress was of amethyst satin embroidered with silver and sewn with a great many pearls in honor of her sister. The silver embroidery scratched her neck and arms and her crown was rather tight as well as being too heavy, and altogether she was very glad when the ceremony was over, the last slice of wedding cake had been cut and the last handful of rose petals had been thrown after the bride and bridegroom's crystal coach.

"Well, that's *that!*" said the Ordinary Princess, tossing her crown onto her bed and wriggling out of her amethyst satin bridesmaid's dress.

She fetched an apple from the top shelf of her book shelf where she kept a hidden store of them, and perched herself on the windowsill of her room in her petticoat. The evening sun was making the treetops of the forest all dusty gold, and there was a great twittering among the birds.

"I suppose next year it will be my turn to get married," thought the Ordinary Princess. "Oh dear! I'm sure I shan't like it a bit. No more fun. No more forest. Having to wear best dresses every day. Crowns and court curtseys and state banquets and things like that. No climbing trees, and a very handsome husband with no sense of humor!"

The Ordinary Princess sighed gloomily and threw her apple core at some rabbits.

"Your Highness!" cried Nurse Marta in a shocked voice, bustling into the room with a great rustling of her starched skirts. "Sitting at the window in your petticoat! Whatever will you be doing next? Suppose someone were to see you!" She hustled the Ordinary Princess away, drew the curtains, and lit all the lamps.

"But Marta, it's still daylight," said the Ordinary Princess wistfully, "and there's such a lovely sunset."

"What has that got to do with it?" asked Nurse Marta. "It's past seven o'clock and that is quite time to draw the curtains." And she scolded the Ordinary Princess for leaving her beautiful bridesmaid's frock on the floor— "Your Highness! Your Highness!" said the old nurse, throwing up her hands in horror, "when will you learn to behave like a princess?"

Then she called the ladies-in-waiting and the maids, and they all chattered and laughed together like a flock of starlings as they brushed the Princess

Amy's hair and poured scented water into her marble bathtub.

"Now there is only one princess," said her ladies-in-waiting. "Soon there will be suitors coming for Your Highness, and next year there will be another wedding." But the Ordinary Princess only yawned. She wished they would not talk so much, for it had been a very long and tiring day, and she had a headache. Besides, she was not very interested in weddings: she had been a bridesmaid at six of them, and by now it all seemed a little dull.

But very soon it began to look as though there was not going to be a seventh wedding after all.

The King became flustered and peppery and the Queen became more and more anxious and distracted as time went on. The Prime Minister and the Lord High Chamberlain and all the Councillors of State went about with such long faces that the Ordinary Princess said it was a wonder they did not trip over their chins.

It was not that there was any lack of suitors. The fame of the princesses of Phantasmorania had gone abroad, and each year princes and peers had come from all over the wide world to make offers of marriage. There were quite as many as, if not more than, the numbers who had paid visits of ceremony at the palace of Phanff in the year before the wedding of the Princess Pearl. For was there not still one princess left? And didn't everyone know that youngest princesses are always the most beautiful and charming of all?

The court of Phanff, you see, had always been discreetly silent on the subject of its seventh princess, and outside the kingdom it was naturally supposed that the Princess Amethyst was as beautiful, if not more beautiful, than any of her six lovely sisters. So of course the list of visiting suitors was as impressive as ever.

One after another, as the months rolled by, princes and Grand Dukes and Royal Highnesses and Serene Transparencies of every description, shape and size arrived at the palace of Phanff to pay a friendly visit, but in reality to meet Her Serene and Royal Highness the Princess Amethyst Alexandra Augusta Araminta Adelaide Aurelia Anne of Phantasmorania. But none of them ever stayed more than one day.

One after another, after their first shocked look at the Ordinary Princess, they hurriedly remembered previous engagements. They apologized for having to make such a brief stay and said that if they should ever happen to be passing that way again they would of course drop in. After which they would pack their luggage and hurry away the very next morning.

None of them ever stayed a second day, except His Serene Transparency the Archduke of Pantechniconia, who was in such a hurry to leave that he tripped on his ermine-trimmed cloak on the top step of the grand staircase and fell down the whole flight. After which, of course, he was so bruised that he had to be put to bed for a week before it was safe for him to travel.

So the year went round and the winter passed, and it was spring once more. And once again it seemed to the Ordinary Princess as though the sky had fallen into the Forest of Faraway, as she lay on her back in a sea of bluebells and watched a pair of orioles building their nest in the branches over her head.

As she lay there, she sang to herself a nursery rhyme that her ladies-in-waiting used to sing to her when she was a little girl. It is a very old song now, but then it was almost new . . .

"Lavender's blue," sang the Ordinary Princess,
"Rosemary's green,
"When you are King
"I shall be Queen."

No one listening to her would have realized, from her lighthearted singing, what a very great deal of trouble she was causing. For while the Ordinary Princess lay on her back and sang songs among the bluebells, her father the King was attending an Extra Specially Important Meeting of the Council of State, summoned to discuss the question of the marriage of his last and youngest unmarried daughter.

"Something must be done!" shouted the King.

And he banged on the table so hard that he twisted his thumb and spilled the inkpot onto the Lord High Chamberlain's velvet robe, which did not improve matters.

"It was all your fault in the first place," said the King, getting crosser than ever and finding some difficulty in keeping his crown from sliding over one ear—a thing that always seemed to happen whenever he got in the least excited. "Years ago I sat in this very same room," said the King, sucking his injured thumb, "and warned the lot of you. I warned you that you were being rash—and don't interrupt me, Rodehesia," he added fiercely, turning on the Queen, who had moaned at the sound of that by now all too familiar word.

But the Queen was far too upset to interrupt anyone. She asked for a glass of water and some smelling salts and fanned herself with her lace handkerchief.

"Well?" said the King. "Well? Well? Well? Hasn't anyone got anything to say? Has no one any ideas?"

The Council maintained a gloomy silence, and the Queen took a sip of water and said in a faint voice, "We must do *something*. The disgrace of it! There has never been a spinster in all the Annals of the Phanffarias."

The Prime Minister coughed apologetically.

"Well, Your Majesty," said the Prime Minister, "there has never been a princess in the family quite . . . er . . . quite like . . . er . . ." He caught the King's eye and subsided.

"I asked for *ideas*," said the King tartly, "not criticism. What I want from all of you is less criticism and more ideas. Her Majesty is quite right. No princess of our house has ever before failed to make a brilliant marriage. *And,*" added the King, looking fiercer than ever, "we are not going to start now!" He raised his fist to thump on the table, thought better of it, and glowered at his councillors instead.

There was a lot more silence.

"Well?" demanded the King again. "Well? Well?"

"If I might make a suggestion, Your Majesty," said the Lord High Chamberlain nervously, "could we not try the effect of a . . . er . . . dragon?"

"On whom?" inquired the King, puzzled.

"Er . . . on the suitors, Your Majesty. It has sometimes proved very useful in the case of—er—er—not very attractive young damsels," he finished hurriedly.

"Explain yourself," ordered the King sternly.

"Well, Your Majesty knows what romantic minds these young princes have, so suppose we hired a dragon to—to lay waste the countryside—?" (Here the Minister of Public Safety looked alarmed and the Minister for Agriculture and Fishery was heard to protest.) "We might then imprison Her Royal Highness in a tower and send out a proclamation to say that any prince who slew the dragon should be rewarded by the princess's hand in marriage. I venture to think, Your Majesty," said the Lord High Chamberlain more nervously than ever, "that this might have the—er—desired effect. Provided, of course, that Her Highness was kept—er—out of sight as it were," finished the Lord High Chamberlain rapidly.

"How *can* you say such a thing? Oh, my poor child!" wailed the Queen, taking a long sniff at her smelling salts. But the King suddenly sat up straight with a wild look in his eye.

"I believe there's something in it," said the King.

The Council brightened visibly, and the Lord High Chamberlain tried hard to look modest. "To think," said the King, "that after all these years, one of my councillors should actually have had an idea. You," said the King, pointing at the Prime Minister, "will see to it at once that a special committee is formed to carry out the project. We will require a Minister in Charge of Hiring a Suitable Dragon and a sub-committee for drawing up the draft of a suitably worded proclamation. And you, my dear," said the King turning to his Queen, "will please see to it that Amy retires to a secluded tower and remains there, out of sight, until this affair reaches a happy conclusion."

The King rubbed his hands together and beamed cheerily at the relieved Council. "A capital scheme!" he said. "I've yet to hear of a prince who could resist the chance of killing a dragon. Some silly young nitwit is sure to come charging up to slay the creature, and then," said the King, "we'll have him! He simply can't turn the girl down after that. And anyway," finished the King cheerfully, "he won't see her until it's too late!"

"But what about Rubarbary?" inquired the Queen at this point.

"Eh?" said the King.

"Her Majesty means His Royal Highness the Grand Duke Reginald of Rubarbary," put in the Prime Minister helpfully. "Perhaps Your Majesty forgets that His Highness arrives this afternoon for the express purpose of seeing Her Highness the Princess with a view to matrimony?"

"*Tcha!*" said the King. "We all know perfectly well by this time what will happen as soon as he lays eyes on her." He scratched his chin and looked thoughtful. "I suppose," said the King hopefully, "we couldn't say that she had a chill and see if he'd make an offer for her hand without seeing her?"

"I fear, Sire, that such a ruse would only cause His Highness to prolong his visit until he *did* see her," said the Prime Minister.

"Perhaps you're right," said the King. "Well, as we can't possibly produce any dragons by this afternoon, we'd better give Amy one more chance of getting off without one. And if the Grand Duke remembers a previous appointment after seeing her, then we'll try this dragon scheme of yours. Come, my dear," and straightening his crown, the King went merrily off to take a stroll in the kitchen gardens. He was a man of simple tastes, and his hobby was growing onions.

That evening, before the banquet for His Royal Highness the Grand Duke Reginald of Rubarbary, the Queen paid a visit to the apartments of her youngest daughter.

"Now please pay attention, Amy," said the Queen, sitting down on the edge of the Ordinary Princess's golden bed, "because this is very important. I particularly wish you to make a good impression on the Grand Duke, for if he should take a fancy to you, it will save your Papa and myself a great deal of trouble. And—er—expense," added the Queen, thinking of the high cost of hiring dragons.

"Yes, Mama," said the Ordinary Princess.

"So you will please put on your most becoming dress and your prettiest crown."

"Yes, Mama."

"And for goodness' sake, child, don't stand like that! Feet together, please. And remember to stand up straight and answer nicely when you are spoken to. And look as if you were enjoying yourself."

"Yes, Mama."

"Do please try and remember to keep your back to the light as much as possible. I have heard," said the Queen hopefully, "that His Highness is a little shortsighted, and I can only trust that it is so. Always bear in mind that you are a princess of the royal house of Phanffaria, and even if you are not beautiful, try and look as though you were."

With which puzzling remark Her Majesty departed.

But, alas, in spite of all her good advice, the evening was a failure from the start.

His Royal Highness the Grand Duke of Rubarbary was not only pudgy and pompous but full of pride, and the Ordinary Princess took an immediate dislike to him from the moment he entered the room. All her royal Mama's eyebrow signals and all her royal Papa's whispers of "Amy, behave!" could not make her be more than stiffly polite to him. While as for the Grand Duke, all the best dresses and becoming crowns and shortsightedness in the world could not disguise from him the excessive ordinariness of the Ordinary Princess.

"Good gracious!" said the Grand Duke in a very

loud whisper to his guard, "I don't believe the girl's
a princess at all. Who ever heard of a princess with
hair that color? And her *nose*, Count Poffloff. Have
you noticed her nose? Freckles—positively freckles!
Shocking!"

So the banquet was not a success, even though the
Grand Duke Reginald ate a great deal and seemed,
by the noise he made, to enjoy his food. The Ordinary
Princess sat at his right hand, but she did not talk
to him at all; firstly because she did not want to,
and secondly because his mouth was always full, so
he did not look as though he could have answered
her if she had.

After this, no one was in the least surprised to
hear, when the banquet was over, the Grand Duke
telling the King how sorry he was not to be able to
stay a second day, but he had just remembered
a promise he had made to visit the Baron Boris of
Bigswigsburg and that he was afraid he would have
to leave immediately after breakfast next morning.

"I knew this was going to happen," said the Prime
Minister glumly as he went off to look up the price
of hiring dragons.

A week went past, and then one day, when the
Ordinary Princess was playing by herself in the forest, she met a party of girls from the city of Phanff
who had come to the forest to picnic and gather
bluebells.

The Ordinary Princess had taken off her shoes and
stockings and tucked up her gown above her knees

to keep it out of the damp moss, and no one would ever have suspected her of being a Royal Highness! The picnic party certainly did not, and as she was a friendly sort of person, in a few minutes they were all talking and laughing together as though they had known each other for years.

They climbed trees and ran races and picked enough bluebells to fill every apron with flowers. But when the sun began to sink behind the distant horizon, they said they must go home.

"Oh dear," said the nicest girl (her name was Clorinda and she was just as freckled and jolly as the Ordinary Princess), "it's sad to think that this is probably the last time for months that we shall be able to come out here and pick flowers and enjoy ourselves."

"Why do you say that?" asked the Ordinary Princess. She had hoped that they might come again soon, for they were nice, laughing, cheerful girls and not a bit like the fine ladies of the court.

"Haven't you *heard?*" asked the one whose name was Phyllida. "The Council of State is getting in a dragon to lay waste the countryside, and once the creature arrives it won't be safe to go outside the city walls."

"Whatever do you mean, 'getting in a dragon'?" demanded the Ordinary Princess. "Do you mean on *purpose?* But whatever for?"

"It's on purpose all right," nodded Clorinda. "You must come from some very out of the way village if you haven't heard about it. It's because of the princess, you know."

"The princess!"

"Yes. You see, nobody wants to marry her because she's not pretty as princesses go."

"But the dragon?" insisted the Ordinary Princess. "Go on about the dragon. Whyever a dragon?"

"Well you see, it's this way," said Clorinda, plumping herself down on the moss and quite willing to explain. "The King and all the old councillors think that if they hire a dragon to lay waste the countryside, and keep the princess shut up in a tower where no one can see her, they can send out a proclamation to say that whoever kills the dragon can marry her. Well, you know what princes are," said Clorinda wisely. "Just a lot of little boys when it comes to killing dragons. So of course some prince will get all heroic and kill the poor creature, and as soon as he does he'll simply have to marry the princess. See?"

"I see," said the Ordinary Princess.

"It may be all right for the King," said Clorinda, "but I must say, I think it's bad luck on his kingdom." She got up off the moss and began filling her apron with the bluebells she had picked. "No more picnics," she said sadly. "And the dragon is sure to kill some poor villager's cows and sheep before it gets killed itself. I think it's a shame."

"Yes," agreed the Ordinary Princess. "You're right, Clorinda. It is a shame. And what's more, it ought to be stopped. And I know how to stop it!"

"What's that?" asked Clorinda, who had been busy with her flowers.

"Nothing," said the Ordinary Princess. "I was only thinking aloud. I say, Clorinda . . . would you do something for me?"

"Surely," said Clorinda. "What is it?"

"You're about my size," said the Ordinary Princess, frowning thoughtfully. "Will you swap your dress for mine?"

Clorinda looked a bit doubtful.

"Come on," urged the Ordinary Princess. "Just for fun."

"Well—" said Clorinda, "I suppose it's all right. But that's an awfully pretty dress you've got on— much nicer than mine."

"Then that's settled," said the Ordinary Princess. "Come on, behind that tree trunk."

A few minutes later there came out from behind the tree a princess in a plain homespun dress and a print apron, and a girl in a trailing gown of amethyst-colored brocade.

"Here are my shoes and stockings," said the Ordinary Princess, pulling them out of a hollow oak where she had hidden them. "I say, we do fit each other's clothes well, don't we?"

"It's a simply lovely dress," sighed Clorinda, stroking the brocaded folds. "I didn't realize it was such a grand one, the way you had it all bunched up. I've always wanted one like this . . . are you sure you don't mind?"

"Of course not. I've always wanted one like *this*," said the Ordinary Princess. "You'd better run, Clorinda—your friends have started."

"Oh goodness," cried Clorinda. "I must fly! Good-bye."

"Good-bye," called the Ordinary Princess.

She stood at the edge of the forest waving her hand until Clorinda was out of sight. Then she turned and looked up at the walls and towers of the palace.

"Dragons!" said the Ordinary Princess. "I'll give them dragons. So they think they can push me off on to any silly prince who kills a dragon, do they!" And she stamped her foot and stuck out her tongue at the palace walls just to relieve her feelings. "*Well, you just wait and see!*" she said.

When she was safely back in her room, she took off Clorinda's dress and apron and Clorinda's buckled shoes and cotton stockings and hid them behind the amethyst-colored tapestries on the walls. Then she put on one of her own embroidered gowns and went demurely down to supper.

After supper she said she was tired and would go to bed early. But as soon as Nurse Marta and the ladies-in-waiting had gone, she got up again, lit one of the scented wax candles, and wrote a short letter.

She propped the letter up in a conspicuous place on the mantel and dressed herself in Clorinda's clothes. And because it was rather cold, she took her plainest cloak as well. Then she climbed out of the window for the last time.

There was a full moon, and the forest looked all black and silver and mysterious in the moonlight. But it did not frighten the Ordinary Princess, because she knew it too well and was so fond of it.

She stopped where the trees began, to wave her hand at the turrets and towers and glistening walls of her home. Then, turning her back on it, she plunged into the forest and was gone.

The next day the uproar in the palace was beyond description.

The flight of the Princess Amy had been discovered by her two ladies-in-waiting, whose duty it was to wake her each morning. But on that particular morning they found that there was no one to wake. The big golden four-poster bed with its amethyst satin draperies was not only empty but had obviously not been slept in, while on the carved marble mantel stood a square white envelope on which was written in large block capitals:

TO WHOM IT MAY CONCERN

The ladies-in-waiting evidently thought that it concerned them, or perhaps it was just that their curiosity became too much for them. Anyway, they opened it at once, and when they read the letter inside they both screamed at the top of their voices, and one of them fainted away. The one who didn't faint called for help and then ran as fast as she could to the Queen.

The King and Queen were having breakfast together in the sun parlor when the lady-in-waiting burst in on them. She was breathless with excitement and also because she was rather plump and had been running very fast down a great many corridors. "Oh, Your Majesty!" gasped the lady-in-waiting, panting like a goldfish out of water, "Oh, Your Majesty!"

"Good gracious!" exclaimed the King, dropping his spectacles into the butter. "Is the place on fire?"

But the lady-in-waiting merely burst into tears and handed the princess's letter to the Queen.

It was a very short letter, and this is what it said:

Dear Everyone,

I think this dragon idea is simply silly and I won't be shut up in a tower, and what's more I won't marry any stupid dragon-slaying prince. In fact I've decided that I don't think I'll marry anyone ever, so I've run away and it's no use trying to find me, and please don't worry because I shall be quite all right.

Love and kisses
Amy.

There were several spelling mistakes.

The Queen read it, and when she came to the end, she screamed even louder than the two ladies-in-waiting put together and went off into a fit of hysterics. The King knocked over the coffeepot and spilled a new jar of marmalade in his agitation, and search parties were rushed off in every direction with orders to find the princess and bring her back immediately.

But nobody saw so much as the flicker of her skirt.

The Ordinary Princess had vanished as completely as though she had been made of snow and had melted away in the sunshine.

The King fined all his councillors half a month's salary to relieve his feelings, and the Minister in Charge of Hiring a Suitable Dragon had to write and cancel his order for: Dragons, I. Laying-waste-the-land; for the use of.

PART III

When You Are King

The Forest

"I really shall have to do something about my clothes," said the Ordinary Princess, speaking rather severely to Mr. Pemberthy and Peter Aurelious.

Mr. Pemberthy and Peter Aurelious had not the least idea what she was saying, but they tried to look intelligent and sympathetic.

Mr. Pemberthy was a little red squirrel and Peter Aurelious was a crow.

The Ordinary Princess hardly ever had anyone to talk to, so she had made friends with the forest creatures and talked to them. It tended to make conversation rather one-sided, but that was sometimes an advantage. At least they could not answer back!

The little red squirrel and the bright-eyed crow had become so tame that the Ordinary Princess gave them proper names (she had called the squirrel after a jolly, red-haired pastry cook at the palace, and the

crow after her Uncle Aurelious), and now they followed her everywhere and came when she called them.

It was a fine sunny morning on the far side of the forest from the kingdom of Phantasmorania, and the Ordinary Princess was gathering wild strawberries for lunch. Nearly two months had gone by since the night she had scrambled down the wisteria outside her window and run away into the forest, and every day had taken her farther and farther away from her home, until after weeks of wandering she had reached the other side of the great Forest of Faraway and the borders of the kingdom of Ambergeldar.

The open-air life seemed to agree with her, for though she was thinner, she was as brown as a berry and her cheeks were as rosy as the little wild crab-apples. But for all that, on this particular morning she was wearing a rather worried frown. The cause of the frown was the question of clothes.

Up to now she had found life in the forest a very simple affair. There were plenty of roots and nuts and berries to eat and water from many little bubbling springs to drink. The forest pools made the most beautiful baths, and the deep emerald moss the most comfortable of beds, and there had not been so much as one rainy day since she left the palace.

Morning after morning the sun had risen in a cloudless sky, and night after night the stars had been friendly candles to light her to bed. But now at last an extremely bothersome thing had cropped up.

Her dress and her apron, once the property of Clorinda, were beginning to fall to pieces, and though nuts and berries may grow on trees, new clothes do not.

Her stockings had been torn to ribbons long ago, and she had lost one shoe in a boggy bit of ground and the other in a stream. But that did not worry her at all, because she liked running barefoot.

But her dress and apron and petticoat were quite another matter.

Wandering in forests, and climbing trees or paddling in streams, are not good for dresses, however sensible their material. "It won't be so long before they fall off in bits," said the Ordinary Princess worriedly.

She had tried pinning the holes together with pine needles and bramble thorns, but it had not been a success: the pine needles broke and the thorns scratched her. Once she had tried to weave herself a skirt of grass and leaves, like people did in books, but that had been a failure from the start. It seemed a good idea all right, but it simply did not work.

"Whatever *am* I going to do?" said the Ordinary Princess to Mr. Pemberthy and Peter Aurelious.

But Mr. Pemberthy was busy eating an acorn, and Peter Aurelious only cocked his glossy black head to one side and said: *"Qwa!"* which might mean anything . . . or nothing.

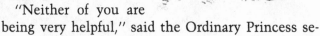

"Neither of you are being very helpful," said the Ordinary Princess severely, and she sat down on a tree stump and ate her strawberries.

When she had finished them, she licked her fingers and went off to a deep pool nearby to wash the juice off her face and hands, and it was while she was drying her face on the least ragged corner of her apron that a cracked voice quite close to her said, "Good afternoon, child."

The Ordinary Princess jumped.

She had not noticed anyone when she came down to the pool, and when she dried the wet out of her eyes, she jumped again, for she saw the oddest sight.

Standing half in and half out of the water, at the other end of the pool, was the queerest old lady she had ever seen. She had long, greenish-gray hair, a long hooky nose, and a pair of very twinkling eyes. She leaned on a stick made out of a knobbly branch of coral and wore a cloak of something that looked like seaweed.

"Speak up, child," said the old lady. "Where are your manners?"

"G-g-good afternoon, ma'am," said the Ordinary Princess. And because she had been nicely brought up, she made the old lady a curtsey.

The old lady gave her a long look from her queer twinkling eyes, and then she said, "You *are* Amethyst, I suppose?"

The Ordinary Princess jumped for the third time and looked a little alarmed. "Yes," she said, "but how did you know?"

"Good gracious, child," said the old lady, seating herself on a lump of rock with the water up to her knees, "I ought to know. I'm one of your godmothers. *I'm* Crustacea."

She gave the Ordinary Princess another sharp look. "You've heard of me, I suppose?"

"Oh yes," said the Ordinary Princess. "I've heard of you. And if it hadn't been for you, Godmama, I wouldn't be here at this minute."

"Does that make you glad or sorry?" asked the old lady.

"Glad!" said the Ordinary Princess promptly. "Though I ought to say," she added truthfully, "that there *have* been times when I've wished I was a really proper kind of princess . . . but not very often."

The old lady laughed a high cackling sort of laugh. "You're a sensible child," she said. "Come and sit beside me and tell me all about it."

So the Ordinary Princess told her the whole story and the Fairy Crustacea laughed and chuckled and wiped her twinkling eyes with the edge of her seaweedy cloak.

"And now," said the Ordinary Princess, "I would like some advice, Godmama. What do ordinary people do when their clothes wear out and they haven't any more?"

"Buy some new ones, child."

"But I haven't any money."

"Then earn some. Go to work," said the old lady.

"Oh, work," said the Ordinary Princess thoughtfully. "I'm not sure I should like that."

"Neither do most ordinary people—but they have to," said the old fairy.

"What sort of work? And where?"

"Great barnacles!" exclaimed Crustacea, "how should I know? Use your head, child. Think for yourself. And as for *where*—well, look over there."

She pointed with her knobbly coral stick and the Ordinary Princess turned and looked.

Beyond the pool the forest ended in a narrow strip of moorland, and between the tree trunks she saw a far distant view of roofs and walls and battlements glinting in the sun.

"Why—there's a town there," she said.

"Certainly there is a town there," said her godmother. "That is the city of Amber, the capital of Ambergeldar, and if I were you, I'd go there and get myself a job. Because one thing is certain," said old Crustacea, "if you go about in those clothes much longer, they will simply fall to bits."

"I was thinking that myself just before I met you," said the Ordinary Princess.

"Then take my advice and go on thinking of it," said Crustacea. "Because the more you think of it, the sooner you will see that there is nothing for it but to buy new ones. And to do that, one needs money. Shops make a point of it, I am told. And money," said Crustacea, "does not grow on trees. So, as you will realize, it all seems to boil down to one word. Work!"

"Work," repeated the Ordinary Princess dutifully. "I expect you're right, Godmama."

"I'm always right," snappd the old fairy. "And now be off with you, child. And luck go with you."

She smiled a very kindly smile, and then, before the Ordinary Princess could even say, "Good-bye," she slipped off the rock and disappeared under the water as smoothly as an otter, and there was nothing to show that she had been there at all, except a damp smear on the top of the rock and a widening circle of ripples on the surface of the pool.

"Well!" said the Ordinary Princess. And she rubbed her eyes and pinched herself to make sure she had not been dreaming. But there were the ripples and the damp smear on the rock, and the pinch had certainly felt very real.

"Anyway," said the Ordinary Princess, "if I've got to start work sometime, I'd better start now."

So she stood up and shook out her ragged skirts and tidied her hair as best she could. Then she went to the tree stump where she had left Mr. Pemberthy and Peter Aurelious and her cloak.

The cloak had not had nearly such hard wear as her dress and apron, for she had used it as a blanket every night and carried it rolled up in a bundle under her arm during the day, and when she put it on, it made her look quite neat and respectable.

"It *is* a pity having no shoes and stockings,"

thought the Ordinary Princess. "But then one can't have everything. Good-bye, forest," she said, "I've had a lovely time, and as soon as ever I've made enough money to buy some new clothes, I'll come back to you!"

She kissed her hand to the trees and the ferns and the emerald moss and set off toward the town of Amber. But she did not go alone, for Mr. Pemberthy and Peter Aurelious had no intention of being left behind.

Mr. Pemberthy had stopped eating acorns and had taken one flying leap onto her shoulder, where he fluffed up his tail and sat looking very pleased with himself. Peter Aurelious flew alongside them, cawing loudly.

It was almost four o'clock by the time they reached the city, and the Ordinary Princess was very tired and footsore. It had been much farther than she had thought when she looked at its walls and roofs from the edge of the forest, which may have been partly because she found that roads are not nearly as comfortable to bare feet as moss, so that one has to go more slowly.

She stopped by a little stone bridge over the river that ran through the town, to bathe her tired and dusty feet and decide what she had better do. "I think I shall try and get work at the castle," thought the Ordinary Princess, wiggling her toes in the nice cool water. She smiled to herself and tweaked Mr. Pemberthy's bushy tail. "It will be a change to work in a castle instead of living in one," she said.

Then she dried her toes on the long grass by the bridge and marched off down the road to the castle.

Perhaps the old Fairy Crustacea's wish that luck would go with her had something to do with it. But strange as it may seem, when she knocked at the back door of the castle and asked for work, she was taken in at once, in spite of that dreadfully ragged gown. For as luck would have it, the fourteenth assistant kitchen maid had tripped over the kitchen cat that very morning and twisted her ankle. So the Ordinary Princess got the job at two pfennigs a week, plus her keep and the loan of a spare apron.

"How many pfennigs would it take to buy a new frock?" she asked the thirteenth assistant kitchen maid.

"About a hundred," said the thirteenth assistant kitchen maid. "But it depends on the frock."

So that is how Her Serene and Royal Highness, Amethyst Alexandra Augusta Araminta Adelaide Aurelia Anne, Princess of Phantasmorania, became an ordinary kitchen maid in the royal castle of Amber.

She was soon to find out that a great deal of work was expected in return for two pfennigs a week and her keep.

From early dawn until late at night she was busy scampering up and down the huge castle kitchens, washing dishes, peeling potatoes, fetching and carrying for the royal cooks, filling pails of water, and a hundred other things.

At night she slept in a narrow rickety bed in a very small attic room at the tip-top of the castle. The bed was very hard and the mattress full of lumps, but she was always so tired that she did not care.

Whenever she could snatch a moment from her work, she would run up the twelve long flights of stairs that led to her attic, to take a handful of crumbs and scraps to Mr. Pemberthy and Peter Aurelious.

Mr. Pemberthy and Peter Aurelious spent most of their time sunning themselves on the castle roofs or making trips down to the gardens. But wherever they were, the minute they heard the Ordinary Princess's soft whistle they would hurry back to the attic windowsill.

Every second week the Ordinary Princess was allowed Thursday afternoon off, and then all three of them would spend a glorious time together in the forest. And every Saturday night the Ordinary Princess would put two pfennigs into a cardboard box with a hole in the lid that she kept under her bed.

"When the box is full," she told Mr. Pemberthy and Peter Aurelious, "I shall take it down to the town and buy myself a new frock, and then we can all go back to the forest and live there for always. Or at least," she added, "until I need a new one."

Peter Aurelious put his head on one side and said, "*Qwa!*" and Mr. Pemberthy fluffed up his tail and made a little chattering noise, quite as though they both understood what it was all about. Which perhaps they did.

On the whole, the Ordinary Princess—who was now an ordinary kitchen maid—enjoyed life as much as ever. For when you have spent most of your life surrounded by ladies-in-waiting and polite courtiers who all expect you to do nothing but play the harp nicely and do a little elegant embroidery, even peeling potatoes has its charms. And there is nothing that gives you a feeling of such proud satisfaction as drawing a weekly wage that you have earned all by yourself. Even if it is only two pfennigs!

Every now and again the Ordinary Princess would send a letter to her parents, to tell them that she was quite safe and well and happy, so that they would not worry about her too much. But she was very careful to give no address, and as no one used postmarks in those days, she was never discovered.

The Ordinary Princess had been an ordinary kitchen maid for several weeks before she caught so much as a glimpse of the castle's owner, King Algernon of Ambergeldar. But though she had not seen him, she had heard a great deal about him from the other seventeen assistant kitchen maids.

It seemed that he was young and gallant and handsome and that his mother had died when he was only a baby, and his father had been killed out hunting when he was ten years old, so he had been a king since that early age.

The kitchen maids, the scullery maids, and the

housemaids, the scullions, pages, cooks, and serving maids were never tired of talking about him, and to hear them one would suppose him to be the most marvelous person in the world.

"But they can't fool *me*," said the Ordinary Princess to Mr. Pemberthy and Peter Aurelious. "I know *all* about kings and princes. They may seem very wonderful to kitchen maids, but believe me, when you get to know them, you'd be surprised how stiff and stodgy and tiresome they are."

She spoke so snappishly that Mr. Pemberthy looked quite startled and dropped an acorn.

"*Algernon*, indeed!" said the Ordinary Princess in tones of immense scorn.

"*Qwa!*" agreed Peter Aurelious.

The cardboard box with the hole in the lid contained the sum of twelve pfennigs when the whole castle was thrown into a bustle of excitement. It seemed that Queen Hedwig of Plumblossomburg was to pay a friendly visit to her nephew, Algernon of Ambergeldar, and great plans were made to receive and entertain her.

"Friendly visit my foot!" said the thirteenth assistant kitchen maid, whose name was Ethelinda. She was sitting on the steps of the kitchen yard in the sun, helping the Ordinary Princess to shell peas.

"You mark my words," said the thirteenth assistant kitchen maid darkly, "it's that there Persephone!"

"What do you mean?" asked the Ordinary Princess. "And who is Persephone?"

"The Princess Persephone, that's who! Queen Hedwig's daughter. You see, it's this way," explained

Ethelinda, only too willing to stop shelling peas and gossip instead. "Queen Hedwig, who's coming to visit here, is the King's aunt. And her daughter, that there Persephone who is the King's cousin, is coming with her. *Now you mark my words*," repeated Ethelinda impressively, "she's bringing that girl of hers along in 'opes, as you might say."

"In what?" asked the Ordinary Princess, puzzled.

"H-o-p-e-s, 'opes," said the thirteenth assistant kitchen maid, who tended to forget her aitches when excited. "She'd not 'arf like to see her daughter Queen of Ambergeldar."

"Oh, I see," said the Ordinary Princess. "That kind of hopes. I know those!"

"That's it," said Ethelinda, absentmindedly eating raw peas. "It's policy. Or that's what I think they call it. Something like that." She smiled rather condescendingly at the Ordinary Princess and added, "Of course *you* wouldn't understand. Not having been long in royal circles, as you might say. But let me tell you, dear, the Fuss there is over princes and kings and princesses and such-like getting married you wouldn't 'ardly believe."

The Ordinary Princess only just stopped herself from saying, "Oh, wouldn't I!" She got as far as "Oh" and stopped there.

"Fuss ain't the word for it," continued the thirteenth assistant kitchen maid, her mouth full of peas. "Why, the princesses that have come here on 'friendly visits' would fill this here yard twice over and still leave some outside. It's them councillors if you ask *me*," said Ethelinda wisely. "They're always at him to get married. Badgering, I calls it. Plain *badgering*. That Prime Minister is always inviting princesses to stay at the castle. Gives us a lot of extra work it does. But he hasn't fallen in love with any of 'em yet!—the King, I mean."

The thirteenth assistant kitchen maid gazed across the kitchen yard and sighed sentimentally. "I suppose he will one day," she said sadly. "Not that no one would be good enough for 'im. Coo!" sighed the thirteenth assistant kitchen maid, "don't I just wish I was a princess!"

On the first night of Queen Hedwig's visit there was to be a magnificent ball in her honor, and the Ordinary Princess and all the other castle servants were hard at work before the sun rose that day.

The Queen was bringing with her a retinue of more than a hundred knights and courtiers and ladies-in-waiting with their servants, pages, and men-at-arms. Every room in the castle was full, while the overflow camped in tents of damask in the castle gardens, so that the lawns looked like a gaily colored fairground.

The Ordinary Princess had managed to escape from the kitchen for a few minutes when no one was looking, and from a corner of the castle battlements she had seen the royal visitors ride in procession through the great gateway. Soldiers presented arms, drums rattled, cannon boomed, and banners and pennants fluttered in the breeze.

Queen Hedwig rode on a white horse with glittering trappings, and four knights in armor held a golden canopy over her head. The Ordinary Princess thought she looked very proud and bossy and disagreeable.

Behind her, carried in a jeweled chair, came the Princess Persephone. She was as beautiful as the evening star, but she bowed and smiled in a rather bored sort of way—like a mechanical doll, thought the Ordinary Princess—while the people cheered and threw rose petals into her lap.

The Ordinary Princess would have liked to wait and see some more, but she was afraid to stay longer in case one of the cooks should notice that she had gone. So she slipped away and went back to the very sticky and tiresome job of stoning cherries.

That night, when the big yellow moon rose over the treetops and shone down upon Amber Castle, nobody noticed it at all. For the castle and its gardens and park, and all the city, was illuminated in honor of Queen Hedwig's visit, and there was such a blaze of light that the moonlight seemed faint and wan.

In the state rooms of the castle thousands upon

thousands of sweet-scented wax candles glowed from golden candlesticks, or glittered from chandeliers, while out in the gardens hundreds of gaily colored lanterns swayed among the branches of the trees and hung like strings of jewels along the clipped yew hedges. It really was the most entrancing sight. But lovelier and more splendid than the colored lights or the glittering crystal chandeliers were the noble guests in their wonderful satins and brocades, all stitched with gold and silver thread and winking with jewels, as they walked to and fro in the lantern-lit garden.

The Ordinary Princess hung out of her attic window at an extremely dangerous angle and admired it all very much.

She had really only stolen up for a few minutes to bring some almonds for Mr. Pemberthy and a handful of cake crumbs for Peter Aurelious. But the sound of music and the buzz of voices from the garden below had brought her to the window, and there she had lingered, quite entranced by the lovely sight.

Not that she had much use for state balls as a general rule, having already danced at too many, dressed up in stiff and scratchy gold-encrusted gowns and wearing her heavy for-very-best-occasions crown. But tonight she thought it would have been fun to wander in that lantern-decked garden or to dance to the fiddles across the shining ballroom floor. For high as her attic was, she could hear the music plainly, and the musicians were playing a tune that she knew well:

"Lavender's blue," played the fiddles,

"Rosemary's green,
"When you are King
"I shall be Queen."

The Ordinary Princess sighed and ran back to the kitchens, where she got a good scolding from the second assistant cook for being away so long. And after that she found no further opportunities to creep away and watch the revels.

The music and the dancing lasted until long after midnight, and the moon was sinking behind the chimneys and gabled roofs of the town by the time the last minuet had been played and the wheels of the last coach had rumbled out of the castle yard.

One by one the footmen and the servingmen, the cooks, the scullions and the scullery maids drifted off to bed.

The kitchen maids went last of all, and the Ordinary Princess found herself alone with the dying embers of the fire on the big kitchen hearth.

She had stayed behind the others to see if there were any nuts left over from the dessert that had been served at the banquet. (Mr. Pemberthy was *extremely* fond of nuts!)

She searched among the piles of half-empty dishes that were stacked on the scullery tables, but there did not seem to be any nuts. "I know," thought the Ordinary Princess, "I'll go up to the banquet hall. There won't be anyone there now, and I'm sure they won't have cleared everything away—that will be done in the early morning."

She ran down the long stone passage and up the back staircase that led from the royal kitchens to the state apartments. The castle was very quiet, deserted and still, and the Ordinary Princess went on tiptoe. The candles had all burned out, and only the low moonlight came in through the tall windows.

She crossed the marble hall where the servingmen had waited between courses, and pushed open the big double doors of the banquet hall. The doors were made of cedar wood, all carved and gilded, and they were so heavy that the Ordinary Princess had to push her hardest to open them.

The banquet hall had not been cleared. The long tables were still littered with golden dishes half full of sweets, nuts, and candied fruit, empty wine glasses, and tired roses in crystal bowls.

On one of the tables the candles were still burning. And on the edge of the table, swinging his legs and licking strawberry ice cream out of a silver ladle, sat a young man who could only be one of the senior royal pages.

He was a nice-looking young man in a wine-colored velvet doublet and with rather tousled hair. The Ordinary Princess stopped just inside the door.

"Hello," said the nice young man.

"Hello," said the Ordinary Princess.

They looked at each other in the candlelight, and the nice young man smiled.

It was a nice smile that made his eyes crinkle up at the corners, and the Ordinary Princess smiled back.

She had a rather nice smile herself, and it wrinkled her freckled nose.

"Were you looking for something?" inquired the young man.

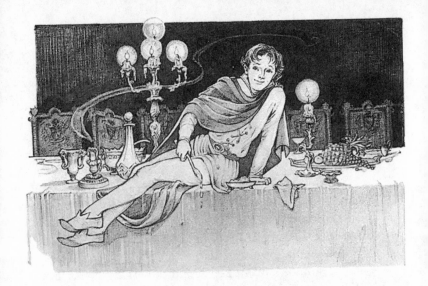

"Nuts," said the Ordinary Princess. "For Mr. Pemberthy," she explained.

The young man looked puzzled. "Mr. Pemberthy?"

"He's only a squirrel," said the Ordinary Princess, "but he's a particular friend of mine, and he is *extremely* fond of nuts."

"Oh, I see," said the nice young man, quite as if he did.

"I thought there might be some left over, so I came up to look," explained the Ordinary Princess. "But I didn't expect to find anyone here."

"If it comes to that, neither did I," said the nice young man. "But as we're both here, why not have some ice cream? I can recommend it." And he pushed away some of the dishes and made room for her on the table.

"It does look good," said the Ordinary Princess, "but do you think we ought to?"

"Certainly!" said the nice young man. "Who's afraid! Will you have strawberry, vanilla, raspberry, or chocolate?"

"Strawberry, please," said the Ordinary Princess, perching herself on the table beside him.

"There aren't any clean plates left," said the nice young man, handing her a frozen spoonful, "so you'll have to lick. But, personally, I always think it tastes better that way, only one is never allowed to do it."

"Perhaps that's why," said the Ordinary Princess wisely. "Doing things you aren't supposed to do always seems more fun than doing things you are."

"It sounds a bit mixed," said the young man, "but I'm sure you're right. And now please tell me about Mr. Pemberthy."

So the Ordinary Princess told him how, before she came to be a kitchen maid in the castle, she had lived in the forest and made friends with Mr. Pemberthy and Peter Aurelious and how tame they had become. So tame that when she decided to become a kitchen maid so that she could buy a new dress, they had come with her to the castle.

"And when I have saved a hundred pfennigs," said the Ordinary Princess, "we shall all go back and live in the forest again."

"Why a hundred?" asked the nice young man.

"Well, Ethelinda says that's what a new dress will cost. It sounds an *awful* lot, doesn't it?" said the Ordinary Princess wistfully.

"It depends on the dress," said the nice young man, taking some more ice cream. "How long do you think it will take you to save it?"

"Quite a long time, I'm afraid," said the Ordinary

Princess sadly. "You see I only get two pfennigs a week. But I've got twelve already," she added, cheering up a little.

"Good work," said the nice young man approvingly. "Have some more ice cream."

"Now you tell me about yourself," said the Ordinary Princess after an ice-creamy interval. "What do you do?"

"Oh, I work here," said the young man.

"What sort of work?" asked the Ordinary Princess.

"Anything I'm told to do," said the young man. "I suppose you'd call me a man-of-all-work."

"I thought at first that you were a page," said the Ordinary Princess.

"No such luck. They have a much better time than I do. Two hours off every day, and an afternoon a week," said the young man gloomily.

"Don't you ever get an afternoon off?" inquired the Ordinary Princess sympathetically.

"Hardly ever," replied the man-of-all-work more gloomily than ever.

"Then you ought to *insist* on it!" said the Ordinary Princess indignantly. "I think it's a shame. Even assistant kitchen maids get half a day off every other week, you know."

"What do you do on your half day off?" asked the young man interestedly.

"We go to the forest. Mr. Pemberthy and Peter Aurelious and me—I mean I. One of the cooks lets me take any old scraps of bread and cake that are left over, and we have a picnic. We have a *lovely* time."

She finished the last bit of ice cream in her spoon

and yawned sleepily. "I ought to be going to bed," she said.

"Don't go," begged the nice young man. "It's early yet. Tell me something more about yourself. Did you always live in the forest?"

"Not always," said the Ordinary Princess, "and it's not early. Unless you mean it's early morning, which is quite true. Good night," she said, and she got off the table and made him a rather sleepy curtsey.

"Good night," said the nice young man, smiling his nice young smile.

The Ordinary Princess was halfway up the second flight of stairs to her attic when someone called, "Hey!" in a rather loud whisper.

She turned round, and there was the nice young man again. He must have run after her, because his hair was untidier than ever, and he seemed to be a little out of breath.

"Hi!" said the nice young man. "What about Mr. Pemberthy?" and he held out a handful of walnuts.

"Oh dear," said the Ordinary Princess. "I'd forgotten all about those. Thank you so much."

The nice young man had brought enough to fill both pockets of her apron and to keep Mr. Pemberthy in luxury for several days.

"I say," said the nice young man, getting rather pink, "when did you say your next half day off was?"

"I didn't," said the Ordinary Princess. "But it's Thursday."

"Then may I . . . could I come too?" asked the nice young man, getting pinker than ever. "To the picnic,

I mean. I'd very much like to meet Mr. Pemberthy and Peter Aurelious."

"But do you think they'd let you off?" said the Ordinary Princess.

"Well I'd try—that is, if you'll let me come."

"We shall be delighted," said the Ordinary Princess primly. "Only you'd better not come to the kitchen," she added, "because sometimes I'm late, if it's a very busy day. If you *can* get the afternoon off, I'll meet you by the three silver birch trees at the edge of the forest. You'd better bring your own cake," she said. "Sometimes we don't get very much."

"I'll bring all the cake," said the nice young man.

The castle clock struck three.

"Good gracious!" exclaimed the Ordinary Princess. "It's nearly morning and I have to be up by half-past five! Good night, man-of-all-work."

"Good night, kitchen maid!"

The Ordinary Princess yawned very sleepily indeed and went off to bed.

PART IV

I Shall Be Queen

"The Birches"

The Ordinary Princess was feeding the last of the cake crumbs to Peter Aurelious and watching the man-of-all-work making a necklace out of acorn cups strung on a grass stem.

The evening sunlight was throwing long shafts of gold between the mossy tree trunks of the forest, and all around them birds were singing in the green thickets.

"This has been quite the nicest day of my life," thought the Ordinary Princess. And she thought, too, that the nice young man was easily the nicest person she had ever met. "It's because he is an ordinary sort of person—like me," she decided.

And indeed a more ordinary person than the man-of-all-work you could not wish to see. His velvet doublet was stained with moss and rather torn where he had caught it on a branch while climbing an oak

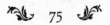 75

tree to pick acorns. His hair was very ruffled and full
of bits of bark, and he had a smudge on his nose. As
he strung the acorn cups on the grass stem, he whis-
tled softly to himself . . .

"*Lavender's blue,*
"*Rosemary's green,*
"*When I am King*
"*You shall be Queen.*"

"There!" he said, finishing the necklace and dropping it into the Ordinary Princess's lap. "Be careful
of it or it will break."

"It's simply lovely," said the Ordinary Princess,
"and I shall keep it for ever and ever!"

"I don't expect it will last *that* long," laughed the
man-of-all-work. He lay back against the green moss
and the twisty tree roots and gazed up happily at the
crisscrossy pattern of branches over his head.

They had had a beautiful afternoon. The Ordinary
Princess had managed to get away early from the
castle, and as soon as she came within sight of the
three silver birches on the edge of the forest, she saw
that the nice young man was already there, waiting
for her. He told her that he had been able to get the
afternoon off without too much trouble, and he had
brought a basket full of cakes, sandwiches, and apples.

He made friends at once with Mr. Pemberthy and
Peter Aurelious, and after hiding the basket under
a wild rose bush at the foot of an old oak tree, they
had all gone off into the forest to explore. Later they
had climbed trees and played at ninepins with fir

cones and crabapples. The young man had also shown the Ordinary Princess how to lie flat on the bank of a stream with her arm in the water and flip the little silvery, slippery trout out from under the stones and onto the grass.

Together they had caught five, and though they had thrown them all back at once, they had both got very wet, moss-stained, and excited and had enjoyed themselves enormously.

Mr. Pemberthy had visited his friends among the treetops, and Peter Aurelious had hopped and pecked and flown around among the bushes.

When teatime came round, they picnicked under the biggest oak tree they could find and laughed and talked together as if they had known each other for always.

"Kitchen maid," said the nice young man suddenly, flipping an acorn at the Ordinary Princess, "what is your name?"

"Amy," said the Ordinary Princess, catching the acorn neatly and handing it to Mr. Pemberthy.

"Nice name. It suits you," said the nice young man, adding in tones of immense scorn, "Persephone, indeed!"

"Who?" said the Ordinary Princess, rather startled.

The young man looked a little confused.

"I was only thinking," he said, "what silly names some people have. Why, I should like to know," inquired the young man hotly, "can't more people have nice, sensible, pretty names like Amy?"

"I suppose you mean the Princess Persephone," said the Ordinary Princess. "I don't know why it is, but princesses always *do* seem to have rather fussy names. You couldn't imagine a princess called Amy, now could you?"

"I don't see why not," said the nice young man. "Perfectly good name for anyone. I know we haven't been properly introduced, but I shall call you Princess Amy."

The Ordinary Princess smiled to herself.

"And what shall I call you?" she asked.

"My friends call me Peregrine," said the nice young man.

"Well, I'm your friend, aren't I?" said the Ordinary Princess, and she stood up and held out her hand to him.

"Of course," said Peregrine the man-of-all-work, jumping up and taking it.

So they shook hands and laughed at each other.

"Peter Aurelious and Mr. Pemberthy," said the Ordinary Princess, "permit me to introduce you to a friend of mine—Peregrine."

"*Qwa!*" said Peter Aurelious politely.

"Princess Amy," said the man-of-all-work, "allow me to present a friend of mine—*Prince* Peregrine."

"I am honored, sir," said the Ordinary Princess, sweeping an elegant court curtsey.

"You said that just like a real princess," laughed Peregrine.

The Ordinary Princess straightened up from her curtsey rather hurriedly and said that it was high time they started back to the castle. "Look!" she said. "You can see the evening star already."

And sure enough, the sun had gone down, and between the tree trunks of the forest they could see the evening star twinkling in the apricot-colored sky above the distant rooftops of the city.

"We shall have to hurry," said the Ordinary Princess, "or we shall be dreadfully late and get locked out when they close the castle gates at sundown. Besides, I'm on duty after dinner."

So they ran back to Amber in the twilight and arrived at the back gate that leads to the kitchen quarters quite breathless and very dusty.

"May I come and picnic with you and Mr. Pemberthy and Peter Aurelious this day fortnight, if I can manage to get off again?" asked Peregrine.

"Do," said the Ordinary Princess.

"Then I'll meet you at the three silver birch trees again," said Peregrine, "and I don't know when I've enjoyed myself so much before. Good night, Princess Amy."

"Good night, Prince Peregrine," said the Ordinary Princess, and she slipped through the back gate and vanished into the kitchen.

After that the hardest or messiest work never seemed quite so hard or so messy to the Ordinary Princess. The days seemed to fly past, and she would sing to herself as she scoured pots and pans, peeled potatoes, or washed dishes . . .

> *"Lavender's blue,*
> *"Rosemary's green,*
> *"When you are King*
> *"I shall be Queen."*

She sang it so gaily that even the grumpiest cook had to smile.

Every second Thursday she would fetch Mr. Pemberthy and Peter Aurelious, and they would all go off to meet Peregrine by the three silver birch trees at the edge of the forest.

They spent the most delightful afternoons exploring and paddling in the pools and streams. Peregrine made her a bow and arrows out of willow stems and taught her how to shoot at a circle that they cut with his penknife in the bark of an oak tree.

One day he brought a large bundle under one arm, as well as the picnic basket.

"What's that?" asked the Ordinary Princess.

"Wait and see," said Peregrine.

When they reached their favorite oak tree, he opened the bundle. Inside was an axe, a little saw, a box of long nails, a hammer, and some rope.

"I thought it would be fun to build ourselves a house to picnic in when the winter comes," said Peregrine.

The Ordinary Princess clapped her hands with joy.

"You do have the *nicest* ideas of anyone I know," she said. "Now where shall we build it?"

In the end they chose a lovely spot in a tiny open glade in the forest. Two silver birch trees grew in the middle of it, and a little spring bubbled out of the moss close-by. They cut stout branches of oak, beech, and fir, sawed them into proper lengths, and hammered them deep into the earth to make the walls. Across these they nailed other pieces of wood and made a roof of willow branches, pine boughs, and ferns.

They worked tremendously hard and got very hot, breathless, and happy.

It took several second Thursdays before it was finished, but at last it was done. They had carpeted the floor of the little house with the brightest green moss they could find and had cut more squares of moss to thatch the roof. The house had two windows and a door that opened and shut. And though the windows had no glass in them and the door did not lock, that did not worry them at all. They were extremely proud of their work.

"What shall we call it?" asked the Ordinary Princess. "Don't let's call it anything palacey or castleish. Let's give it a nice ordinary sort of name."

"Let's call it 'The Birches,'" said Peregrine. "That's ordinary enough, and besides, there are two silver birches right beside the door."

So "The Birches" it became, and next time they came to the forest Peregrine brought a bottle of ginger ale with him, and the Ordinary Princess smashed the bottle over the door, exactly as she had seen her royal Mama smash bottles of champagne over the prows of her royal Papa's new ships, and said, "I name you 'The Birches.'"

The ginger ale trickled down the door and soaked into the moss, and Peter Aurelious tried to drink it.

Autumn had come again, and in the forest the leaves were turning red, amber, and gold, and the thickets were full of blackberries, hazelnuts, rosehips, and thorn apples. But at the castle Queen Hedwig and her daughter the Princess Persephone still stayed and stayed. It did not look as though they were *ever* going to leave.

"I do wish to goodness they'd go, or that the King would make up his mind and marry her, or something," said the Ordinary Princess one day to Peregrine.

"Why?" asked Peregrine—his mouth rather full of blackberries.

"Because having so very many visitors makes an awful lot of extra work for kitchen maids," sighed the Ordinary Princess. "You wouldn't believe how much! And Ethelinda says that Queen Hedwig won't go until she's managed to marry her daughter to King Algernon."

"Perhaps he doesn't want to marry her," said Peregrine, taking another mouthful of blackberries.

"Well, she's awfully pretty," said the Ordinary Princess. "I saw her once. Haven't you ever seen her up close?"

"Once or twice," said Peregrine.

"What's she like?"

"Like a princess," said Peregrine.

The Ordinary Princess threw a very squashy blackberry at him and hit him on the nose. "That's a silly answer," she said.

"No it isn't," said Peregrine, wiping blackberry juice out of his eye. "I've worked at the castle for quite a long time, and if you'd seen as many princesses as I have, you'd know what I mean. They are almost as alike as peas in a pod!"

The Ordinary Princess smiled a little secret smile to herself and said, "Tell me about princesses, Perry."

"Well, first of all, they are very beautiful," said Peregrine, leaning back against a tree trunk and ticking off the points on his fingers. "Then secondly and thirdly and fourthly, they all have long golden hair, blue eyes, and the most lovely complexions. Fifthly and sixthly, they are graceful and accomplished. Seventhly, they have names like Persephone, Sapphire, and Roxanne. And lastly," said Peregrine, running out of fingers, "they are all excessively proper and *extremely* dull . . . except when they are make-believe princesses who are really kitchen maids!"

"That's just what I've always thought about princes," said the Ordinary Princess.

"All of them?" asked Peregrine.

"All except the make-believe ones who are really men-of-all-work," said the Ordinary Princess.

Then they both laughed and went back to the castle hand in hand.

Now just about this time it happened that the Ordinary Princess's old nurse, Marta, came to the city of Amber on a visit to her sister's niece, who had married a merchant of Ambergeldar.

Nurse Marta's sister's niece had a large and jolly family of children who loved going for picnics, and Nurse Marta's sister's niece's husband was particularly fond of blackberry-and-apple pie. So one late autumn day, when there was beginning to be a nip in the air, Nurse Marta and her sister's niece, and her sister's niece's husband, and all eight children went picnicking in the forest to collect blackberries.

Now Nurse Marta was rather stout and short of breath, so instead of rambling through the forest with the others, she sat herself down on a nice comfortable clump of grass with her back to a tree trunk.

In spite of the time of year, the sun was very warm that day, and there was not a breeze stirring in the forest. Nurse Marta dozed.

And so it happened that the Ordinary Princess, coming running round the tree trunk, tripped over Nurse Marta's feet and fell right into her lap!

"Help!" cried Nurse Marta, waking up very suddenly.

"I *am* so sorry," apologized the Ordinary Princess, picking herself up. "I didn't know that anyone was—" She stopped rather quickly. "Why, Marta!" gasped the Ordinary Princess.

"Mercy me! Your Highness . . ." gasped Nurse Marta. "Oh, Your Highness!"

"Oh do hush, *please!*" begged the Ordinary Princess.

But it was too late. "What's all this about Highnesses?" asked Peregrine, who had been running after her. They had been playing tag.

"Nothing," said the Ordinary Princess hurriedly. "Nothing at all. I—I think this old woman has made a mistake," and she frowned very hard at Nurse Marta.

But her old nurse was far too excited and upset to take any notice of mere frowns.

"Oh, Your Highness, wherever have you been!" she cried. And she caught the Ordinary Princess in her arms and kissed her and hugged and cried over her. "We thought you were lost! Oh, Princess Amy, how *could* you, my lamb? Your dress! It's got holes in it—and no shoes on; you'll catch your death of cold! What *would* your royal Mama say if she could see you now!''

She went on and on, and the Ordinary Princess could do nothing to stop her, until at last she ran out of breath and sat down heavily among the tree roots and wrung her hands.

By which time, of course, it was far too late to pretend anymore, and the Ordinary Princess patted Nurse Marta's plump shoulder and said that she was quite all right and that if Nurse Marta would write down her address she would come and see her and explain everything.

So when Nurse Marta had stopped panting, she gave the Ordinary Princess her address, and having promised faithfully not to breathe a word of the affair to anyone, she curtsied several times in an agitated sort of way and went off between the tree trunks still wringing her hands.

After she had gone, there was a long silence.

The Ordinary Princess was looking rather ashamed of herself, and Peregrine was frowning.

Presently he said, frowning more than ever, ''So you were a real princess all the time. Amy, you are a little fibber! And for two pins,'' said Peregrine, ''I'd give you a good hard spanking!''

The Ordinary Princess stopped looking ashamed of herself and giggled instead.

''You can't spank a Royal Highness,'' she said.

''*Can't I!*'' said Peregrine, looking quite as if he could.

But the Ordinary Princess tugged at his velvet sleeve with her little blackberry-stained hand and said, "But it's not *my* fault, Perry! I can't help being a princess. And anyway it doesn't make any difference, does it?" she added anxiously.

"No," said Peregrine, and he smiled his nice smile. "It won't make any difference to me. But what about you? You are a Royal Highness, and I . . . I'm only a man-of-all-work."

"What does that matter? I should like you every bit as much if *you'd* turned out to be a—a coal heaver!" said the Ordinary Princess hotly. "So there!"

"I'll remember that when I'm a coal heaver," promised Peregrine. "And now suppose you sit down and tell me how it is that a princess came to be a kitchen maid."

So they both sat down on the moss and the fallen leaves, and the Ordinary Princess told him all about everything, right from the very beginning. And he laughed such a lot that they quite forgot the time and had to run all the way back to the castle, for fear of being locked out when the gates were shut.

"Good night, Prince Peregrine," said the Ordinary Princess, slipping in at the back door.

"Good night, kitchen maid," called Peregrine.

"Qwa!" said Peter Aurelious.

Mr. Pemberthy said nothing at all, because he was sound asleep already, curled in a little furry ball in the Ordinary Princess's apron pocket. He continued to sleep so soundly that she hadn't the heart to disturb him, so she hung up her apron on a hook in her cupboard and went down to help with the dishwashing without it.

There appeared to be more dishwashing to be done

than *ever* that night. The piles of greasy dishes seemed as if they reached the ceiling. The Ordinary Princess broke three dinner plates and was severely scolded by the fourth assistant senior cook, whose temper was never very good.

You have to pay attention when washing dishes, what with the slipperiness of wet plates, and the Ordinary Princess did not have her mind on plates! She was wondering whatever she was going to say to Nurse Marta.

"Oh dear," thought the Ordinary Princess, "why did she have to come and spoil it all?"

She sighed heavily and dropped a soup plate.

It broke into eighteen quite small pieces, and one of these flew up and caught the fourth assistant senior cook on the nose.

As we already know, his temper was not of the best, and what with so much extra work, on account of Queen Hedwig of Plumblossomburg and her daughter and all her attendants staying on and on, and a bad attack of toothache that had been keeping him awake for the past three nights . . . Well, the end of it was that the Ordinary Princess found herself dismissed.

The fourth assistant senior cook did not put it as elegantly as that.

"You're fired!" shouted the fourth assistant senior cook. "Take a week's wages!" And with that he had ordered her out of the kitchen.

"I don't care!" said the Ordinary Princess, climbing wearily up the fourth flight of stairs on her way to the attic. "I don't care a *bit!*" and a large tear rolled down her cheek and dripped off the point of her chin.

"Oh dear, oh dear," sobbed the Ordinary Princess, sitting down suddenly on a step. "Whatever *am* I going to do now?"

Someone was whistling somewhere . . .

> "Lavender's blue,
> "Rosemary's green . . ."

"Hi!" called Peregrine in a loud whisper, appearing unexpectedly at the bottom of the staircase. "I've been waiting to catch you. There was something I wanted to say."

But the Ordinary Princess went on sitting on the stairs, while her tears splashed onto her shabby dress.

Peregrine came up the stairs four steps at a time.

"I say," he said, "what's happened?"

"I've been f-f-fired!" sobbed the Ordinary Princess.

"You've been *what?*"

"D-d-dismissed," wept the Ordinary Princess. "I b-broke f-f-four plates, and Cook f-f-fired me!"

"Good!" said Peregrine approvingly.

"How *can* you say that?" flared the Ordinary Princess. She stamped her foot and suddenly stopped crying. "How can you be so horrid when you know quite well that I haven't saved *nearly* a hundred pfennigs and I don't know where I am to get another job."

"Darling Amy," said Peregrine, "don't cry. I only said 'Good' because I think it's awful, your having to work so hard. You shall have all the pfennigs you want and all the dresses in the world!"

He lent her his pocket handkerchief, and the Ordinary Princess mopped her eyes, blew her freckled nose, and sniffed.

"I'd have given you a hundred pfennigs weeks ago," said Peregrine, "only I was afraid that if I did, you'd just buy a new dress and run off to live in the forest, and I should never see you again."

He smiled his nice smile at her, and the Ordinary Princess could not help smiling back. Suddenly she felt much better.

"You see," began Peregrine—but just at that moment a door on the landing below opened, and through it came a very gorgeous person indeed.

He wore a suit of crimson and violet taffeta, all laced with gold and embroidered with twinkling jewels, and wherever there was room for one he seemed to have added a bunch of ribbons. The toes of his purple velvet shoes were quite half a yard long, and he carried a tall golden stick.

"Now we shall catch it!" thought the Ordinary Princess, for she was quite sure that tearful kitchen maids and sympathetic men-of-all-work were not supposed to sit about on staircases and gossip—even on back staircases.

The very gorgeous person stood quite still and stared at them. His face got redder and redder until it was almost purple, and his eyes seemed as though they would pop out of his head in horror and amazement.

"Oh my goodness," thought the Ordinary Princess frantically, "now Perry will get into hot water too, and I shall be fired all over again."

But it seemed that the very gorgeous person was not going to fire anyone, for quite suddenly he stopped staring and getting purple, and bowed very low instead.

"Your Majesty must excuse me," said the very gorgeous person, bowing again, this time even lower than before, "but I was to request Your Majesty's presence in the Council chamber. One of Your Majesty's guards informed me that you had been seen coming this way, and though I could not believe . . ."

Here the very gorgeous person broke off and gave an apologetic sort of cough, bowed again, and said humbly, "I trust I do not intrude, but the Prime Minister begs to remind you that the matter is urgent."

And with a shocked look at the Ordinary Princess (who really was looking *very* like an ordinary kitchen maid!) he bowed himself backward through the door.

"Well!!!" said the Ordinary Princess.

"Of course this *would* happen!" said Peregrine.

"Well I must say!" said the Ordinary Princess, and without saying it, she rose and started up the stairs in a very stately manner.

Peregrine put out a hand and caught the hem of her skirt.

Since it is almost impossible to continue walking up a staircase in a stately manner while someone is holding onto your dress, the Ordinary Princess stopped and said very haughtily indeed, "Will Your Majesty be so good as to release me."

"Don't show off!" said Peregrine. "I can talk just like that too, if I want to. And I *was* going to tell you. I really was. That's what I waited for. Only of course that flatfooted fathead of a Court Chamberlain had to go and spoil it all."

"So you were a real prince—I mean king—all the time," said the Ordinary Princess.

"Yes," said the King. "I'm afraid I was."

"For two pins," said the Ordinary Princess severely, "I'd give you a good hard slap!"

The King grinned at her cheerfully.

"You can't slap a king," he said.

"*Oh can't I!*" said the Ordinary Princess, quite as if she could.

Then they both laughed so much that they had to sit down on the stairs again.

"Why did you tell me that your name was Peregrine?" asked the Ordinary Princess.

"Well, you must admit that 'Algernon' is pretty awful," said the King. "Besides, my name *is* Peregrine. At least, it's one of them. I've got eight altogether. And between you and me," said the King, "the other six are pretty awful, too!"

"I've got seven," said the Ordinary Princess, "and some of them are simply terrible."

And at that they laughed so much that they had to hold onto each other to keep from slipping off their step.

"This is dreadful of us," said the Ordinary Princess, drying her smudged face with the edge of her shabby skirt. "We can't go on just sitting here and laughing. Someone will catch us. And besides, prime ministers and councils don't like being kept waiting."

"Let 'em wait," said the King cheerfully.

But the Ordinary Princess got up from her step and dusted her frock.

"You may be a king," she said, "but kings are men-of-all-work too!"

"I was trying to forget it," said the King.

"Good night, man-of-all-work," said the Ordinary Princess.

"Good night, kitchen maid," said the King.

So the Ordinary Princess ran up to her bed in the attic, and the King went off to the royal Council chamber.

The councillors were yawning and fidgeting, because they had been waiting for quite a long time for the King, and anyway they hated night sessions. It made bedtime so late. But as the Lord Chamberlain had said, the matter under discussion was an urgent one, so when the King arrived, they all stopped yawning and looked rather severe, though their bows were as low and as correct as ever.

"Gentlemen," said the King, sitting down on the gilded throne at one end of the Council chamber, "you may be seated."

There was a rustle of robes as the councillors sat down again. "And now," said the King cheerfully, "what's the trouble?"

The trouble, it seemed, was the question of the King's marriage. The Prime Minister had called a Council of State to urge His Majesty to ask for the hand of Her Royal Highness the Princess Persephone of Plumblossomburg, and now, in speeches that lasted fully an hour and a half, the Prime Minister, the Chancellor, and the Secretary of State for Foreign Affairs pointed out the advantages of the match . . .

What a good thing it would be for the kingdom to have a queen. What an excellent thing it would be for the country to have such a rich and powerful ally as Plumblossomburg. How greatly it would encourage trade, and how beautiful and gracious and charming and cultivated was the Princess Persephone.

Some of the older councillors frankly dozed, and the King played tic-tac-toe with himself on a bit of blotting paper.

He had tried to interrupt once or twice, but the Prime Minister, the Chancellor, and the Secretary of State for Foreign Affairs all had good loud voices, and as they were absolutely *determined* to finish their speeches, he gave it up and went on playing tic-tac-toe and trying not to yawn.

The fact of the matter was that the entire Council had got so used to managing affairs while he was a little boy that they sometimes forgot that he was a little boy no longer and quite capable of thinking for himself. But by now they had all told him what to do and how to do it for so long that everybody had become used to it. So the King continued to play tic-tac-toe, until there was no more room on the blotting paper and the Prime Minister and the Chancellor and the Secretary of State for Foreign Affairs had run out of things to say.

When they had quite finished, the King tore up his piece of blotting paper and stood up.

"Gentlemen," said the King, "I have listened with the deepest interest to all that you have had to say." (Which was really *far from true*, but royalty has to tell this kind of fib sometimes.) "And may I say," continued the King, "that I am deeply touched by your concern for my welfare." (Royalty has to talk like this too.) "But," said the King, suddenly ceasing to be quite so royal, "I'm dashed if I'll propose to Cousin Persephone."

"*Your Majesty!*" gasped the Prime Minister, the

Chancellor, the Secretary of State for Foreign Affairs, and all the councillors at once.

"Don't interrupt me," said the King. "I have listened to all your speeches, and now you can jolly well listen to one of mine. I am going," said the King, "to marry Her Serene and Royal Highness the Princess Amethyst of Phantasmorania, with or without your permission. So there!"

"But Your Majesty—"

"I haven't finished yet," said the King severely. "I desire an embassy to set out for Phantasmorania immediately, to ask King Hulderbrand for his daughter's hand in marriage. And the sooner," said the King, "the better. That's all I wanted to say."

With which he bowed politely to the assembled councillors and marched off to bed.

"Phantasmorania!" said the Prime Minister.

"It *is* an idea," mused the Chancellor.

"Well, *really!*" said the learned councillors.

"Whatever will Queen Hedwig say?" groaned the Secretary of State for Foreign Affairs.

"I say," said the King, reappearing rather suddenly round the door, "I forgot to mention that I think one of you should drop a hint to Her Majesty my aunt that even the most friendly of visits ought to end some time. She and my cousin and all the ragtag and bobtail they brought with them have been here for weeks and *weeks*," said the King severely, "and it makes a lot of extra work for the kitchen maids!"

And with that he disappeared round the door again, leaving the Council gasping with dismay.

The Prime Minister was the first to recover.

"You know," said the Prime Minister, "that idea

of the King's about an alliance with Phantasmorania is not a bad one. I don't know why we didn't think of it before. It is every bit as powerful as Plumblossomburg—with whom we are already connected, Queen Hedwig being the King's aunt. And come to think of it," said the Prime Minister thoughtfully, "she is undoubtedly a very bossy sort of woman, and if our King married her daughter, she would probably be an almost *permanent* visitor in the Castle . . .

"Yes," decided the Prime Minister, "it is obviously all for the best. Chancellor, kindly see about drawing up a draft for the hint that His Majesty requested, and the rest of you had better start think-ing about an embassy to King Hulderbrand."

The next morning, when the Ordinary Princess woke up, she found a note that had been pushed under her door. It said, "Meet me at the summer-house by the lily pond as soon as possible. Urgent. P." So as soon as she was dressed, the Ordi-nary Princess ran down-stairs and let herself out through a side door of the castle.

She went round by the kitchen gardens, past the greenhouses and cold frames, and came through a back way into the castle gar-dens by the royal lily ponds.

It was a cold morn-ing, and there was frost on the castle lawns and a thin, glittering rim of ice round the edge of the lily ponds, and though it was early, someone was earlier still. Inside the summerhouse, someone was whistling, "Lavender's blue."

"I thought you were never coming," said the King.

"It's a dreadfully cold morning, so I've brought a warm cloak for you."

"I came as soon as I could," said the Ordinary Princess, snuggling gratefully into the cozy folds of the fur-lined velvet cloak.

"Now look here," said the King, "I haven't much time, as I'm supposed to be having breakfast with my Aunt Hedwig, and afterward there is so much state business to attend to this morning that this is the only time I could get off. So pay strict attention to what I'm going to say."

"All right," said the Ordinary Princess. "I'm listening."

"Well, first of all," said the King, "will you marry me?"

"*Perry!*" gasped the Ordinary Princess.

"Yes or no," demanded Peregrine.

"Oh Perry!" laughed the Ordinary Princess. "*What* a way to propose!"

"There isn't time for a proper one," said Peregrine. "I have to be with Aunt Hedwig at eight o'clock sharp, and as this is going to be a particularly annoying day for her, I don't want to make matters worse by keeping her waiting for her breakfast."

"But marrying a king is a very serious business, you know," the Ordinary Princess pointed out. "Don't you think I ought to have a little time to consider it?"

"No," said Peregrine. "You told me yourself that you'd like me just as much if I turned out to be a coal heaver—remember?"

"But you didn't turn out to be a coal heaver, did you!"

"That's not the point," said Peregrine. "What I want is a plain yes or no."

"Then are you sure that you don't mind freckles and turned-up noses and mouse-colored hair?"

"I love them!" said Peregrine. "Yes or no?"

"Yes," said the Ordinary Princess promptly.

"Darling kitchen maid!" said Peregrine, catching her into his arms and kissing her. "I knew you wouldn't desert me. Then *that's* all right. And now to business. You can't go on being a kitchen maid, and anyway, you've been fired. So you can't go on staying here."

"Why ever not?" asked the Ordinary Princess.

"Well, first of all because I'm sending an embassy to ask your father for your hand, all properly, and it would be a bit awkward for everyone if you weren't there. Secondly, we can't go letting the populace find out that their future queen was once an assistant kitchen maid at the castle, because populaces are awful snobs, you know, and I don't think they would ever recover from the shock."

"I expect you're right," agreed the Ordinary Princess forlornly. "I shall have to go back."

"I'll come for you as soon as I can," promised Peregrine.

"But that won't be for months," said the Ordinary Princess more forlornly than ever. "You know what *ages* they take arranging things and fussing over royal weddings."

"I know," said Peregrine gloomily, "but I'll tell the embassy to hurry things up as much as possible. In the meantime I think you had better go off at once to Nurse Marta's, and I'll come there as early as ever I can tomorrow morning, to take you home. We can ride through the forest and no one will ever know."

"All right," said the Ordinary Princess. "There's the quarter-to-eight bell! You'll have to run. Goodbye, Perry darling, and don't let your Aunt Hedwig bully you too much."

She watched the King's long legs disappearing round the clipped yew hedges and sighed.

"He *is* a dear!" thought the Ordinary Princess, "and I suppose I'm glad he is a king and everything is going to end happily ever after. But I still think that sometimes I shall be just the littlest bit sorry that I wasn't a real kitchen maid and he wasn't a man-of-all-work. It *has* been such fun," sighed the Ordinary Princess. And she wrapped the splendid cloak more closely around her and went back to the attic to fetch Mr. Pemberthy and Peter Aurelious, before leaving the castle by the tradesmens' entrance, to go in search of Nurse Marta.

Very early the next morning, before the sun was up, Peregrine came to Nurse Marta's sister's niece's house to fetch the Ordinary Princess.

Nurse Marta's sister's niece had lent her a clean dress and apron and a pair of buckled shoes, and she wrapped herself up in the fur-lined cloak that Peregrine had given her.

"Good-bye," said the Ordinary Princess, kissing Nurse Marta. "Hurry up and come back soon—and don't ever breathe a word about all this, will you?"

She tucked Mr. Pemberthy into her apron pocket, and Peter Aurelious perched on her shoulder.

"What's that?" asked Peregrine as he helped her into the saddle and saw that she was carrying a bundle under one arm.

"It's Clorinda's dress and my old cloak, and the cardboard box with my wages in it. I couldn't bear to part with them," said the Ordinary Princess.

Mr. Pemberthy scrambled out of her pocket and sat on the back of her saddle, and Nurse Marta waved her handkerchief to them from a window as they rode off down the cobbled streets of Amber to the forest, and away to Phantasmorania.

There is a shortcut through the Forest of Faraway to the city of Phanff in Phantasmorania, and though travelers by the highroads take at least three days to get from one kingdom to another, by riding hard all day through the forest Peregrine and the Ordinary Princess came to the palace of Phanff by moonrise.

They halted their horses at the edge of the trees, and Peregrine helped the Ordinary Princess to dismount. She was a little stiff from so much riding and very cold and depressed.

"I wish I was going back with you," said the Ordinary Princess, holding very tightly to Peregrine's hand.

"So do I," said Peregrine. "But don't let's think of that. Let's think of what fun it's going to be when I come and fetch you."

He went with her to the foot of the turret wall where the old twisty stem of the wisteria was just as twisty and knobbly as ever.

"You'll have to throw me my bundle when I'm up," said the Ordinary Princess.

"Good-bye, my kitchen maid," said Peregrine. "Good-bye, my darling Amy. The months will simply fly past, and when the spring comes I will fetch you away."

"Good-bye, my man-of-all-work," said the Ordinary Princess. "Oh, Perry darling, you will take care of yourself, won't you, and don't let your Aunt Hedwig be horrid to you, and don't let them make you marry any tiresome Persephones instead of me, and promise you won't forget me, and I hope that spring comes quickly and I *do* hope I can remember how to climb this thing!" said the Ordinary Princess all in one breath. Then she and Mr. Pemberthy climbed up the wisteria to her turret room, and Peter Aurelious flew up after them.

"Catch!" called Peregrine, and he threw up the bundle which was Clorinda's ragged dress, the old cloak, and the cardboard box with the pfennigs in it.

"Spring will be here in no time," called Peregrine, and he blew her a kiss. Then he mounted his horse and, leading the one that the Ordinary Princess had ridden, turned away in the moonlight and set off into the forest.

You can imagine the sensation there was the next morning when the missing Princess Amy calmly walked down to breakfast as though she had never been away.

Her royal Mama the Queen thought she was seeing a ghost and nearly fainted, and her royal Papa the King said, "Bless my soul!" so many times that it began to seem as though he would never stop.

But when all the flurry and excitement had died

down, they were so pleased to have her back again that they quite forgot to give her the scolding she deserved, in spite of the fact that she looked, if possible, more ordinary than ever.

Certainly she was a good deal thinner. But then she was a little taller too, so that the brocaded gown she had put on did not fit her very well.

"My dearest child!" exclaimed the Queen, throwing up her hands in horror, "whatever *have* you been doing to yourself? I declare you have more freckles than ever. We must do something about them now," said the Queen, bustling off to see about ordering extra lemons and more lily lotion.

"Bless my soul!" said the King, for what must have been at least the fiftieth time. "Well you may look like a gipsy, Amy, but I'm exceedingly glad to see you back!"

"Darling Daddy!" said the Ordinary Princess, kissing the top of his bald head. "I'm glad, too. But no shutting me up in towers and hiring dragons, do you hear?"

"No, no, dear. Not if you don't wish it. Bless my soul!" said the King.

After all the excitement of that first day, they all settled back comfortably into their old lives, and things went on just as before, so that the Ordinary Princess almost began to feel that she had never been away at all and must have dreamed it.

Her Mama the Queen tried as hard as ever to make her look more like a real princess, and the Council of State, who never seemed to learn by experience, tried as hard as ever to find suitors for her hand. The Lord High Chamberlain, an enterprising man (it was he who had suggested the dragon), even went so far as to put forward the name of the Crown Prince Clarence of Kleptomania as a possible husband for the princess. But that suggestion was turned down owing to the unfortunate failing of the Kleptomanian royal family for absentmindedly pocketing any little trifles that might be lying around.

And, as the King said, the disgrace of having an unmarried princess in one's family was preferable to having a son-in-law for whose visits one had to lock away the gold plate and chain the spoons and forks to the table.

"It is quite obvious to me," said the Queen in a resigned voice, "that Amy will be an old maid. There has never been such a thing in our family before, but it seems we are to have one now."

But the Queen was wrong, for a week after the runaway Princess had returned to her home, the Queen came rushing into her turret room in a state of great excitement. In fact she was so excited that it was some time before she could speak.

"My child!" exclaimed the Queen wildly, embracing her youngest daughter. "My Amy!"

She sat down heavily on the Ordinary Princess's golden bed, on top of the Ordinary Princess's second-best dress that had been laid out on the coverlet, and fanned herself with her lace handkerchief while the Ordinary Princess's ladies-in-waiting and maids-of-honor stood around simply bursting with curiosity.

"My child!" exclaimed the Queen again, getting her breath. "Put on your nicest dress at once, and do, my dearest Amy, try to look your best. An Envoy Extraordinary has arrived from His Majesty the King of Ambergeldar to request your hand in marriage! Was there ever such an enchanting piece of news!'' cried the Queen, quite overwhelmed by this unexpected stroke of good fortune.

The King and the whole Council had been equally overcome.

"Do you suppose, dear," said the King nervously, "that they'll change their minds when they see Amy?"

"Leave it to me, dear," said the Queen, and she gave orders that all the lights in the state rooms should be lowered and that only the very plainest ladies-in-waiting should be allowed to attend on the Ordinary Princess.

"That ought to help," said the Queen hopefully.

So the Ordinary Princess was dressed in the most magnificent robes imaginable, and hung with diamonds and amethysts, and made to wear her forvery-best-occasions crown, and sent down to meet the Envoy Extraordinary and his attendants in the throne room, accompanied by the plainest ladies in the palace.

Which probably accounts for the fact that the very gorgeous person whom she had last seen standing at the foot of a back staircase in Amber Castle, and who was one of the Envoy Extraordinary's attendants, never recognized her at all, even though he had stared so hard and so disapprovingly at the little kitchen maid who had been caught talking to the King.

The whole reception passed off beautifully, and when it was arranged that the wedding should take place in the last week of April, the Queen almost wept with joy.

As for the King, he said, "Bless my soul," one hundred and seventeen separate times and raised the salaries of the entire palace staff.

So the Envoy Extraordinary went back to Ambergeldar leaving the court of Phantasmorania quite dazed with excitement, to prepare for the wedding of the seventh princess of the royal house of Phanffaria. But in spite of all the preparations, and the ordering of a most magnificent trousseau, the Ordinary Princess thought that the winter passed slower than any winter had ever done before.

It seemed that spring would *never* come.

Day after day she would sit at her window, looking out at the dark forest where the bare branches of the trees were covered with snow, and wonder if it would *ever* be green again or full of birds and butterflies and wild flowers.

When she was not looking out of the window, she was being fitted for new dresses, or sitting at a desk writing hundreds of "thank you" letters for all the wedding presents that kept arriving at the palace. Then she had to sit for her portrait, as her Mama the Queen had ordered one from Mynheer Van Turpentine, the court painter, to be sent to the King of Ambergeldar, and as nobody dreamed that he had ever seen her, Mynheer Van Turpentine was instructed to flatter her as much as possible. Which he did.

"But it isn't in the *least* bit like me!" protested the Ordinary Princess.

"Nonsense, dear," said the Queen firmly. "It is you at your best. And though I will admit that it is not what one would call a *speaking* likeness, we cannot afford to take any risks. After all," said the Queen comfortably, "by the time His Majesty sees you himself, it will be too late for him to change his mind!" And with that she sailed off to see to the arrangements for displaying the wedding presents.

The Ordinary Princess laughed and tried to imagine what Perry would say when he received Mynheer Van Turpentine's portrait.

"Don't get worried," she wrote to him, "I haven't really grown like that. My nose is still turned up and I have as many freckles as ever."

Peregrine wrote a very correct letter about the portrait to the Queen, but to the Ordinary Princess he wrote, "I have hung the painting in one of the state drawing rooms that I hardly ever have to go into, and when I have to I only think how glad I am that you are not a bit like it and that your nose still turns up and has as many freckles as ever! Darling Amy, don't ever change."

At last, at last, the snow melted and the air became warmer.

Birds began to sing in the Forest of Faraway, and on the boughs of the trees tiny buds appeared and presently the world grew green again. Early primroses spread gay golden carpets between the gray tree trunks, and it was spring once more.

In the last week of April, King Algernon of Ambergeldar, who was also Peregrine the man-of-all-work, came riding to the kingdom of Phantasmorania at the head of a glittering cavalcade of knights, barons and fair ladies. And in the great throne room of the palace of Phanff, His Majesty King Hulderbrand took his youngest daughter by the hand and led her forward to meet the King of Ambergeldar.

"My daughter, Amethyst," said King Hulderbrand, a little flustered by the grandeur of the occasion. "Amy, this is Algernon."

The Ordinary Princess tried hard not to giggle as she swept the most beautiful curtsey.

She was wearing a magnificent gown with a ten-foot train and really looked quite *smothered* in jewels. But the King of Ambergeldar only saw that among the glittering diamonds and ropes of gleaming pearls, Her Serene and Royal Highness, Princess Amethyst Alexandra Augusta Araminta Adelaide Aurelia Anne of Phantasmorania was wearing a little necklace made of acorn cups.

His Majesty of Ambergeldar replied to the princess's curtsey with the most courtly of bows. He was dressed every bit as magnificently as she was and looked very kingly indeed.

"Oh dear," thought the Ordinary Princess in a panic, "he doesn't seem a bit like my Perry!"

Then the heralds blew a fanfare on their silver trumpets, and King Algernon winked at the princess.

"Oh Perry," whispered the Ordinary Princess, under cover of the fanfare, "it *is* you after all!"

"Of course it's me," whispered Peregrine, "but do

try and look as though we've only just been introduced this minute."

"I'll try," giggled the Ordinary Princess, "but I really believe it's the hardest thing I've ever had to do."

And so the next day they were married in the great cathedral of Phanff by twenty archbishops and with the most magnificent of ceremonies.

The Ordinary Princess wore a wedding dress with a train that was seventeen yards long and took twenty pages to carry it. Her six lovely sisters, with their husbands and children, all came to the wedding, and so did the old Fairy Crustacea, who arrived in a chariot entirely made out of oyster shells and drawn by a hundred golden frogs. Her clothes were wetter and more seaweedy than ever, but she was in a remarkably good temper and stayed until quite late.

"I haven't sent you a wedding present," she said as she kissed the bride, "because my presents are not the kind that can be tied up with paper and string.

But bend your head my dear," said the old Fairy Crustacea.

Then she tapped the Ordinary Princess, who was now the Queen of Ambergeldar, on the forehead with her twisty coral stick. "You shall always keep the love of your husband and the respect and devotion of your subjects," said the old Fairy Crustacea. "You shall have four gallant sons and two darling daughters, and you shall live happily all your days!"

"Now *that*," said Peregrine, "is something like a wedding present!"

So Peregrine and his Queen drove away from the palace in a crystal coach, and everyone threw rice and rose petals and satin slippers and waved their hands and their handkerchiefs and cried good wishes.

But nobody noticed that the new Queen of Ambergeldar took with her a rather untidy brown paper parcel, or that perched among the carvings on the coachman's box sat a little red squirrel and a glossy black crow. And of course everyone thought that the royal bride and bridegroom would spend their honeymoon in one of the bridegroom's many castles.

No one guessed that they spent it instead in a little log hut called "The Birches," on the far side of the Forest of Faraway.

For the little hut was still standing in spite of the winter storms and snow. The moss was greener than ever, and primroses, windflowers and wild cherry brightened all the forest.

The Ordinary Princess, who had once been an ordinary kitchen maid and was now Queen Amethyst of Ambergeldar, wore Clorinda's ragged dress, which she had most carefully mended, and cooked the brown trout that Peregrine—who was always Peregrine—caught in the forest streams for their dinner.

Mr. Pemberthy skipped among the branches, and Peter Aurelious cawed happily to himself from the roof of "The Birches."

> *"Lavender's blue,"*

sang Peregrine, chopping firewood,

> *"Rosemary's green,*
> *"When I am King*
> *"You shall be Queen."*

"And so I am!" said the Ordinary Princess.

THE END